Praise for
The Shepherd's Song

"Authors Betsy Duffey and Laurie Myers will engage your heart as you follow Kate McConnell's handwritten copy of Psalm 23 on its journey through the lives of twelve heart-sick people before landing back in the hands of the son for whom it was originally intended. Fast-paced, without rushing their readers, they skillfully bring into view the Good Shepherd, who is able to strengthen the weak, bind up the injured, and bring back the lost (Ezekiel 34:4–6). This book claims to tell of twelve changed lives. Make that thirteen—mine."

—Jani Ortlund, author of *Fearlessly Feminine*
and *His Loving Law, Our Lasting Legacy*,
and executive vice president
of Renewal Ministries

"*The Shepherd's Song* is a powerful collection of stories inter-connected by a single force that has power and strength. Read this fascinating book as seemingly disparate lives are interconnected, not by chance, but by a singular expression of a powerful portion of the Word of God. Prepare for your life to be blessed as you read this wonderful book."

—Frank S. Page, PhD, president and CEO
of the Southern Baptist Convention
Executive Committee

"*The Shepherd's Song* is about an uncommon piece of paper whose travel encircles the globe, providentially changing lives—including the reader's. The message is sutured into the reader's psyche by the masterful use of metaphors, irony, and a never-ending roller coaster of emotions. This single fabric of short stories would make a great movie by an all-star cast."

—Stanley D. Williams, PhD, film producer-director
and author of *The Moral Premise: Harnessing
Virtue and Vice for Box Office Success*

The
Shepherd's
Song

A STORY OF SECOND CHANCES

Betsy Duffey and Laurie Myers

HOWARD BOOKS
A Division of Simon & Schuster, Inc.
New York Nashville London Toronto Sydney New Delhi

Howard Books
A Division of Simon & Schuster, Inc.
1230 Avenue of the Americas
New York, NY 10020

First Howard Books hardcover edition March 2014

HOWARD and colophon are trademarks of Simon & Schuster, Inc.

For information about special discounts for bulk purchases,
please contact Simon & Schuster Special Sales at 1-866-506-1949
or business@simonandschuster.com.

The Simon & Schuster Speakers Bureau can bring authors to your
live event. For more information or to book an event, contact the
Simon & Schuster Speakers Bureau at 1-866-248-3049 or visit our
website at www.simonspeakers.com.

Designed by Davina Mock-Maniscalco

Manufactured in the United States of America

10   9   8   7   6   5   4   3   2   1

Library of Congress Cataloging-in-Publication Data
Duffey, Betsy.
  The shepherd's song : a story of second chances / Betsy Duffey and Laurie
Myers.
    pages cm
1. Christian fiction. I. Myers, Laurie. II. Title.
PS3604.U3739S54 2014
813'.6—dc23 2013017141

ISBN 978-1-4767-3820-8
ISBN 978-1-4767-3822-2 (ebook)

Unless otherwise indicated, all Scripture quotations are from the Holy Bible,
English Standard Version, copyright © 2001, 2007 by Crossway Bibles, a
division of Good News Publishers. Used by permission. All rights reserved.
Scripture quotations marked NIV are taken from THE HOLY BIBLE,
NEW INTERNATIONAL VERSION®, NIV® Copyright © 1973, 1978,
1984, 2011 by Biblica, Inc.® Used by Permission of Biblica, Inc.®
All rights reserved worldwide.

SDG

So is my word that goes out from my mouth:
It will not return to me empty,
but will accomplish what I desire
and achieve the purpose for which I sent it.

—ISAIAH 55:11 NIV

The Shepherd's Song
Psalm 23

The Lord is my shepherd;
I shall not want.
He makes me lie down in green pastures.
He leads me beside still waters.
He restores my soul.
He leads me in paths of righteousness
for his name's sake.
Even though I walk through
the valley of the shadow of death,
I will fear no evil,
for you are with me;
your rod and your staff,
they comfort me.
You prepare a table before me
in the presence of my enemies;
you anoint my head with oil;
my cup overflows.
Surely goodness and mercy shall follow me
all the days of my life,
and I shall dwell in the house of the Lord forever.

The
Shepherd's
Song

CHAPTER

One

The LORD is my shepherd

KATE MCCONNELL opened her eyes. Where was she? There were bright lights above her. Movement. The sound of a siren wailing.

She closed her eyes and opened them again, hoping somehow this all would go away. It didn't.

An ambulance. She was in an ambulance.

What had happened?

A man's voice called out behind her. "Female, age about forty-five, multiple injuries. BP: ninety over sixty. Pulse: one-forty. Respirations: twenty-five, short and shallow."

Each bump and jolt of the ambulance brought pain, crushing pain in her chest and stabs of pain down her right leg. Kate tried to grab her chest, but her arms were strapped down. She shivered uncontrollably. Her blue sweater and pants were covered in something wet—gooey and wet. Blood. He was talking about her.

A brief memory came—her car sliding on the slick road, the sound of breaking glass and crunching metal. *A car accident.* Panic rose in her chest. She had been in an accident.

The newspaper would later say it was the worst traffic accident ever on that section of I-95 between Washington, D.C., and Baltimore—twenty-five cars, six semis, and one bus. The temperature Thursday had been fifty-five degrees, a beautiful day. Then, Friday, it fell to thirty-one, unusual for October. A sudden snow-storm dropped more than two inches of snow in just ten minutes, creating whiteout conditions that took everyone by surprise, including the drivers on I-95.

The voice behind her continued its calm clinical assessment. "In and out of consciousness. Possible head injuries."

"Help," she whispered. Each breath was raw. There wasn't enough air. Dizziness swept over her. She tried again. "Help."

"Hold on. Try to stay awake." A young man leaned over her, making eye contact. His voice was calm, but she saw fear in his eyes.

She tried to nod but couldn't.

"Be still; we're on the way to the hospital."

Everything in her wanted to fight free of the straps and the stretcher, but she couldn't even move her head. Pain radiated from her chest and leg.

The voice began again. "Bleeding profusely from a gash in right leg—looks like an open fracture. Possible in-ternal injuries."

For a few seconds there was silence, the only sound the hum of tires on the road.

"Will do. We'll be there in five to eight minutes, de-pending on traffic."

What had happened? Kate remembered her morning, speeding from one activity to the next, pushing her old station wagon to the point where it shook. An early-morning run to the grocery store, then back home, then a twenty-mile drive to deliver dinner to a friend who was re-cuperating from surgery, then a stop to drop off the dry cleaning, then five more things on her to-do list. Then the snow had started.

The cleaner's. She had been trying to get back to the dry cleaner's, but for what?

She felt a hand on her forehead, and she opened her eyes. The young man's face came into view again. His ner-vous eyes studied her.

"What's your name?"

She tried to focus. Her name?

"Kate . . . McConnell." She gasped out each word.

"Your birthday?"

She tried to come up with the answer, but it was too confusing. Tears welled up.

"It's all right. Just stay with me."

"What hap—?" She wanted to finish the sentence but could not.

"You were in a car accident on the interstate." He held her arm, feeling for a pulse. "There was a pile-up. It's a mess out there."

Her mouth opened and closed with a question un-asked. She wanted to say the words, but nothing came out.

"Matt," she finally gasped out the name of her son. "John." Her husband.

"No one was with you in the car. Just rest and stay calm. We've got you."

She could feel the sway of the ambulance as it passed other cars. The voice faded in and out. She closed her eyes.

A new thought came. She might die. Would it be like this, the end? So fast? With so much undone?

Kate's mind drifted back and forth, weaving in and out of the events of the past week.

"I don't think my life matters," she had told a friend. "I've been a Christian for almost twenty-five years, and I haven't accomplished anything. I can't point to one single person that I've had an impact on, even in my own family."

"Of course you have. You serve on the church worship committee, you deliver meals every week to people in need, and you're always writing down scriptures for people."

"But are those the important things?" Kate had asked. "Do those things matter?"

John. He mattered. And Matt.

"Oh, Mom," she could hear Matt say. "You don't believe all that stuff."

Matt, who had drifted away from faith when he'd started college, now refused to go to church at all.

She couldn't get through to him.

Was she really dying?

Someone lifted her eyelid. It was the young man. He looked closely into her eye, as if he was examining her soul.

"Stay with me now."

She felt the ambulance sway, then the jolt of a sharp turn.

"Help," Kate gasped again as pain stabbed through her side.

"Stay with me."

A wave of dizziness. Then nothing.

———————

JOHN MCCONNELL hovered over the documents on his desk, every ounce of attention focused on the case before him. Behind him shelves and shelves of legal books reached to the ceiling.

"Mr. McConnell. A phone call, line three." His secretary spoke from the doorway.

"I said to hold all calls." He continued scanning the document.

"I know, but . . ."

"I am well aware that we all need to get out of here."

From his twelfth-floor office he had been watching the snow fall. Two inches piled up on his windowsill, and reports of accidents had begun popping up on the Internet.

"Did you finish those edits on the Johnson case?" he asked.

He tried to refocus his attention on the work before him. It was complicated, and now his concentration was broken.

"It's the hospital."

He looked up. Her pale face and wide eyes shattered his calm. A ripple of fear grabbed his stomach. Something terrible had happened. He knew it. He fumbled for a moment with the receiver, then got it to his mouth with shaking hands.

"This is John McConnell."

"This is Metropolitan Medical Center. We have an emergency vehicle on the way."

"Is he all right?" John's voice went up in pitch. His mind was filled with thoughts of Matt. His son was an inexperienced driver, and in this snow . . .

"Mr. McConnell, it's your wife."

"My wife?"

"Yes, Kate McConnell. She's been in an accident. She's being transported here."

"How is she? What happened?" A million questions flooded his mind. He could see Kate as he'd left her that morning, loading the old station wagon with the dry cleaning, recycling, and meals for friends.

"Hey, you're not taking *all* of those, are you?" he had said when he saw her carry out the chocolate cupcakes.

Kate had smiled, dimples showing. "I saved a few for you."

He touched the note that he had found this morning in his briefcase. *Do not be anxious about anything.* Her neat handwriting stood out from the crisp white of the paper.

Kate was a bundle of energy and a bundle of life. How could she be hurt?

"Mr. McConnell? Are you there?"

"Yes."

"We don't have the details, but please come as soon as you can."

"I'm on my way."

Leaving the file on his desk unfinished, John McConnell ran for the elevator.

MATT WAS IN CLASS when he felt his phone vibrate. He considered ignoring it. He was really engrossed in this lecture. The only other thing that could possibly interest him would be the weekend's plans. It was Friday, and he was not yet sure what the next few days looked like. Maybe Joe had gotten tickets for the Rusty Bucket concert. Matt slipped the phone out of his pocket.

Emergency. Call me.

A text from his dad. That was unusual. His dad hardly ever called him, much less texted. Something must have happened. Matt was glad he'd sat in the back. He left his books open on the desk and slipped out into the hall. Did they find the empty beer bottles under the deck? He pressed call. Was he going to have to listen to his father's lecture about drinking and all the legal ramifications?

"Dad?"

Matt steeled himself for the lecture.

"It's your mother, Matt. She's been in an accident. She's on her way to Metropolitan in an ambulance."

Suddenly everything dissolved away: the hall, the classroom, the lecture that he'd been so into. They were gone, and the words coming from his phone were everything.

"Not Mom."

He couldn't take it in.

"Son, it's true. I don't know her condition. Come to the hospital as soon as you can. I'm on my way there now."

Matt couldn't speak.

"Matt? Are you there?" He heard the concern in his father's voice.

"Yeah."

"You okay to drive?"

"Yeah, Dad."

The phone went dead.

Matt stood frozen in place. It couldn't be his mother. She was the strongest person he knew. He had seen her handle difficult situations with ease, and handle several at once. "Mega-Mom," that's what his friends called her. One tiny blond woman, totally in control. He couldn't imagine Mega-Mom in an ambulance. It must be someone else. Someone borrowed her car. Something like that.

He waited for his phone to buzz again, for his dad to call him back and say that it was all a big mistake. What if it wasn't a mistake? No, he couldn't think that. He had to keep it together. He had to get to the hospital.

A BLAST OF COLD AIR hit Kate's face as the ambulance doors opened, jarring her awake. She could hear voices. It came back to her in a rush. The accident. She'd been in an accident. She opened her eyes to movement. People were reaching into the small space around her, all talking at once.

"Kate McConnell, trauma patient."

"Got it. Ready. Lift."

She felt a jar as the stretcher was pulled forward, then lights and swirls of snow. The wheels hit the ground, and they were inside within seconds. Masked faces in white and green hovered over her. Gloved hands touched her.

Two blue eyes looked down at her over a white hospital mask.

"I'm Dr. Belding," a calm voice said. "I'm taking care of you."

The white lab coat was comforting. His white hair spoke of experience. He was in control. No fear in his eyes.

"We are going to fight together," he said. "Stay with me."

The face turned, and the voice changed to business.

"What IV access do we have?"

The paramedic was writing on a clipboard. He answered without looking up. "Eighteen gauge in the right and left arms, both running well."

Dr. Belding grabbed the end of the stretcher and started pushing. "Let's get her to the trauma room and get her intubated."

They moved quickly down a long green hall. They rounded a corner, and the motion stopped for a second like a turning of the tide, then all ahead again, into a spotless room with gleaming metal machines and bins of white sterile packages. Mechanical noises came from all directions, beeping and whirring. The gloved hands moved over her, loosening the straps and cutting away her sweater and pants.

"What's the blood pressure?"

"Seventy over fifty. And decreased breath sounds on the left."

"Open up those IVs."

Kate could not seem to grasp what was happening to her.

"Can you hear me?" Dr. Belding's voice reached into her confusion.

"Can you hear me?" Louder this time. "Give me a thumbs-up."

Kate wanted to lift her thumb, but the slightest movement seemed impossible. She concentrated. She fought with all the determination she could muster. Her thumb went up slightly.

"Good. Let's get some antibiotics on board, and some morphine, too."

Kate's body was not her own. She felt someone open her mouth and put a tube down her throat. *No. No. I'm here,* she wanted to say. *I'm still in here.* She was helpless as chaos swirled around her. In the midst of it all, one kernel of peace came to her. *The Lord is my shepherd.*

Of course. The twenty-third psalm. That's why she had been going back to the dry cleaner's. The psalm had been left in Matt's coat pocket.

A memory came—a vivid picture of herself sitting at the kitchen table, carefully copying Psalm 23 onto a clean white piece of paper. She was writing as neatly and clearly as she could, praying over each phrase. Then she was folding the paper into a square and putting it in the pocket of Matt's wool peacoat. She had imagined him finding it and reading it. How could he not be moved by the promises it held and the clear picture of God as his shepherd?

Instead, anger.

How long would she have to fight with him? And why didn't John help her with the fight?

Now this.

Dr. Belding's blue eyes came into view.

"You can rest now," he said. "We'll take care of everything."

Wait. Who was telling her to rest? She was confused. Did God want her to rest? No. No rest. She had so much to do. She had to get up and get out of here. Her work was not done.

Not yet, God, she prayed. *Please, not yet.*

"THIS IS WBAL REPORTING live from I-95—the scene of the accident." John turned up the volume of his car radio. The light turned green, then red for the third time as he sat in traffic.

"You can hear the helicopters circling as the crash victims are being airlifted out. Luggage and debris are strewn everywhere, blocking the north and southbound lanes." John leaned forward to catch the words.

The snow kept coming down. Big, white, wet flakes piled up on the hood of his car. His wipers thumped rhythmically, keeping a triangle of visibility before him. He fought the rising fear.

"Fifteen reported dead, and many, many others hurt in this horrible crash on I-95. The death toll is rising. If you don't have to go out tonight, just stay home. Now back to the weather."

A horn startled him. The light had changed, and traffic was moving around him. He eased the car slowly through the snowy intersection toward the hospital.

I should pray. "Dear God . . ."

Nothing came. Where was a good prayer when you needed one? Kate was the one who prayed for everyone else. But who prayed for Kate?

The image of Kate lying hurt in the old station wagon came unwanted into his mind. *Don't think.* He must not think. *Why did she keep that old thing anyway?*

"Just get there," he said under his breath. "There will be a way to fix this. There is always a way to fix things." He had learned that in law school. He hoped it was true.

"This is WBAL bringing you news and updates on the worst blizzard in the history of Baltimore."

John punched off the radio and turned his full attention to the road ahead.

———

AS MATT DROVE toward the hospital, he heard the sirens blaring across town. He shivered in his light sweater. Traffic moved slowly, inching through the snow and ice. Matt felt like he was in a dream, moving in slow motion.

It couldn't really be happening. It was all a mistake. When he got to the hospital, they would straighten everything out. They would laugh about it at dinner. He tried to imagine his family, warm and cozy, sitting around the table eating together, making jokes about ambulances and hospitals, but that image wouldn't come into focus.

He tried not to think of his last words to his mother.

He had been so angry. No one had known this morning what the day would bring.

"Come on," he spoke to the traffic in frustration. "Come on."

He made his way around another fender bender, driving carefully, hoping not to slide in the icy slush on the road. His phone buzzed, and he punched it on.

"Dad?"

"Where are you?"

"I'm on my way . . . the traffic."

"Be careful, Matt. It's bad out here. Just take your time."

"Okay, Dad."

His voice broke, and suddenly the first tears came. It was becoming real.

THE LORD IS MY SHEPHERD. The psalm brought peace as Kate lay on the stretcher, helpless to move or speak. She heard the voices around her, but it seemed like a movie or a TV show about someone else.

Dr. Belding maintained a voice you might use while discussing the weather.

"Someone call orthopedics. And let's get an X-ray of that leg. Get an X-ray of the chest, too. And let's get a chest tube in. I think we have a hemothorax."

The pain began to subside as the morphine did its job. Kate drifted.

When she opened her eyes again, she was being wheeled down the long green hall. She heard the voices back and forth over her stretcher.

"What happened?"

"A big pile-up on I-95."

"No kidding. She doesn't look so good. Is she going to make it?"

"You never know with these trauma patients. I've seen ones in worse shape make it . . . but not many."

Kate closed her eyes again. *I might die.* Oddly, now the idea of dying wasn't so frightening or even upsetting. It was just a thought, surfacing in the haze of her mind.

She did not want to leave her family yet, especially after her morning conversation with Matt. His angry face came to mind.

"Mom, I found the psalm you put in my pocket. I wish you'd leave me alone about that." He was slamming his books into his backpack. "You just want to control my life. You always have. Why don't you back off?"

"But, Matt, it's the twenty-third psalm," she had said, as though the significance should be obvious.

"Give it a rest."

"Matt, God wants to be your shepherd. And He is an unbelievable shepherd. He will provide everything you need and protect you and . . ." She knew she should stop talking, but she couldn't.

"Stop it, Mom. Stop it."

"But, Matt—"

"Enough!"

He tossed his peacoat carelessly into the pile going to the dry cleaner's. It wasn't until later, after she dropped off the cleaning, that she remembered the psalm and wondered if it had been in the pocket.

It was strange to worry about the paper now, while she was in the hospital, maybe dying. But she had copied it so carefully and prayed over each phrase. Where was it now?

"Orthopedics just called. They can take her in surgery now."

Dr. Belding grabbed the end of the stretcher. "Okay, people. Let's get her down to the OR." He turned to the nurse. "Has the family been called?"

"They're on the way."

"Good. Let me know when they arrive."

Kate's mind was slowly winding down. The family had been called. John was coming, and Matt.

Take care of them, she prayed. John was so helpless without her. *Take care of them.*

She was moving again. Down the green hall.

Fewer and fewer thoughts made their way into her consciousness. However, the first phrase of the twenty-third psalm played over and over.

The Lord is my shepherd. The Lord is my shepherd . . . shepherd . . .

Ding. Elevator doors opened.

Shepherds take care of their sheep. They feed them. They get water for them. They protect them. They . . .

Ding. Off the elevator. Down another hall. Through double doors. More people. More masks.

The Lord is my *shepherd. . . my own personal shepherd. My very own caretaker. My . . .*

Into a room with bright lights.

She could trust God with her life. She could trust

God to take care of Matt. She could trust God to take care of John.

Peace descended on Kate, and she let go of all struggles.

————

"DAD."

John wrapped his arms awkwardly around his son. For a moment neither could move as they embraced outside the ER.

The sliding glass doors opened, and John and Matt entered a flurry of chaos, pain, and confusion. John moved forward with a surge of confidence. They would go in and figure out what needed to be done. He was good at that. Organizing. Fixing. They hurried toward the information desk.

"I'm John McConnell. You called me. My wife, Kate McConnell, was in an accident."

The attendant behind the counter glanced up.

"Just a minute." Her hair was disheveled, and she had a frantic look as she spoke into the receiver. "Can you hold, please?"

She pushed the hold button and turned to John. "Now, who is it you're here for?"

"Kate McConnell."

John felt his heart pounding in his chest. Time stood still as the woman typed into the computer in front of her. It was taking too long.

"Surgery. They have just taken her into surgery. You can wait in the trauma ICU waiting room. It's on the third floor." She pointed to the elevators.

"Can you tell us anything, anything at all?" John begged.

The girl shook her head. "I'll call the doctor and let him know you're here. You'll have to wait."

That wasn't what he wanted to hear. Waiting wouldn't accomplish anything. He wanted to make strategic phone calls. Contact the right people. That's usually how he solved problems. He thought of the important clients he had. All the powerful people he knew who could get things done with just a phone call. None of them could help him now.

"Dad? What can we do?" Matt asked him.

"Wait."

For the first time in his life John McConnell felt totally helpless.

THE ELEVATOR WAS CROWDED. Matt pushed 3 and immediately began drumming his fingers nervously on his leg. Everything was moving too slowly.

They stopped on the second floor. Doors opened. People got off. People got on.

"Come on."

Finally, the elevator stopped at the third floor, and the doors opened to reveal a distinguished-looking, white-haired doctor.

"You're the family of Kate McConnell?" he asked.

"Yes. I'm her husband," his father answered. "How is she?"

Matt stared at the man in the white coat, trying to read something from his grave expression.

"I'm Dr. Belding. Right now, she is stable. She has a collapsed lung, some broken ribs, and a badly broken leg, which the orthopedic surgeons are working on now."

"So she's going to be all right," Matt said.

Dr. Belding's face maintained the same serious expression. "It's too early to know. Her body has undergone a major assault, and she is very fragile. But we will continue to keep a close eye on her and do everything we can. "

"But she'll be all right." He knew he was almost yelling, but he couldn't stop.

Dr. Belding looked into his eyes.

"We are doing everything we can. You need to be calm and wait."

"When can we see her?" his father asked.

"When she's finished in surgery, they'll bring her to ICU. You can see her then. Wait in there." Dr. Belding pointed to the waiting room. "I'll be back as soon as I know something."

Matt watched Dr. Belding walk briskly down the hall.

As they sat in the waiting room, he kept replaying the argument he'd had with his mother. He could not get comfortable in the vinyl chair.

"Dad?" His father sat beside him leaning forward, his head resting in his hands.

"Yes?"

"Do you think we get second chances?"

His father looked up from his hands.

"I don't know, Matt. I just don't know."

KATE LAY ON THE SURGICAL TABLE. The lights of the operating room were bright above her. Shadows moved about. The only noise was the ventilator slowly breathing in and out, in and out.

The Lord is my shepherd. The Lord. *The Lord God Almighty. The Creator of the Universe.* He *is my shepherd.*

Gentle hands moved her arms into position and covered her with drapes.

Someone whispered in her ear, "I'm going to give you something to make you sleep."

Before Kate's mind went completely blank, she silently sent up a final prayer.

Please, let my life count.

CHAPTER

two

I shall not want

$\mathcal{L}$OVE CAME unexpectedly to Chris Bennett.

It started with a wanting that surprised him with its intensity. He did not see it coming that afternoon as he slid open the glass door of the drive-through lane at Tomasi Cleaners for what seemed like the hundredth time.

Snow fell on his face as he gathered a load of shirts from the backseat of a BMW.

"Monday okay?" he asked over the pile of oxford button-downs.

The driver waved, never stopping his conversation on his cell phone.

Chris loaded the shirts into a garment bag and typed the phone number into the computer. He printed the slip and once again swung the door open to present the tag to the driver. No response. To the customers Chris was invisible. The BMW drove off, and a red Jeep pulled up. Another pile of clothes, another printed slip.

As he sorted the clothes, he fingered a soft yellow cashmere sweater. Noticed the brilliance of a woman's red scarf. Why did some people have so much and others so little? He sorted the clothes, taking care to look for stains and spots, putting the dry cleaning in a separate bag from the laundry.

A memory came from his childhood—a bag of used

clothing that he and his brothers called the "jumble" bag. In the small, dirt-road town of Hayville, a wealthy family would drive through each summer on their way to the lakes for vacation. Chris could see them in their shiny, clean station wagon loaded high with suitcases bound to the top, two perfect children in the backseat providing a stark contrast to the kids playing in the dirt yards of Hayville.

The father would get out and leave the jumble bag on the doorstep of the duplex. The two wide-eyed children would press their faces to the backseat window, watching Chris and his brothers and the others rip open the black garbage bag and dig through the shirts and pants, socks and old underwear. Thinking about it brought back the tightness in his stomach, the scramble for the clothes and the wanting. Everyone trying to get something that fit.

One year he had pulled out a perfect leather moccasin bedroom slipper. But only one. He still remembered the beauty of the soft leather, the perfect fit on his small foot. In desperation he had dug through the bag for the mate, and for years he looked in each jumble bag for the matching moccasin. He never found it.

"Monday okay?" Another load of shirts and sweaters. Another distracted wave.

The snow was really coming down now. His apartment would be cold. There was little food in the fridge. A jar of pickles. A bottle of ketchup. A half-eaten pizza. But he was thankful for his apartment and its furnishings. After years of sharing a room with four brothers, it seemed like a palace.

Chris printed out the receipt for a woman in a black Volvo and opened the door to another blast of cold. He sighed as he turned back and looked around at the mess. It had been a hard day at Tomasi Cleaners—a steady stream of customers all day bringing piles of shirts, jackets, dresses. Endless loads for him to wash and steam and press. He liked working hard and was thankful for the job and the money in his pocket.

He had left Hayville five months ago after he'd graduated from high school. No one was present to see him shake the principal's hand and take his diploma. His mother had been gone since he was a baby, and his father was at work.

Chris had saved $450 from his job in the school cafeteria, a job that gave him free food and some pocket money but earned him the scorn of the other students. It didn't matter. He was happy to leave Hayville and ready to make his way in the world. Even in the act of leaving, though, he stifled the hope inside. He steeled himself for disappointment, as he had all his life.

"It's really coming down out there," Chris called out as he began to sort through the clothes. There were piles everywhere from the rush of customers trying to make it home.

Mr. Tomasi came out of the back rolling a rack of freshly pressed shirts.

"Let's sort the last loads and close early."

Chris nodded. "Looks like it's getting bad."

Chris tackled a pile brought in earlier by Mrs. McConnell. She was such a nice woman. One of the few who didn't look right through him. She would sometimes ask about him. Once she gave him a small card with a Bible verse on it. He couldn't remember what had happened to it.

He separated her laundry from her dry cleaning and began to go through the clothes. He picked up a navy peacoat from the pile. It was nice, probably belonged to her son. Chris looked out the large plate-glass window at the flakes of snow falling steadily now. It was cold out there. The wool coat looked warm. He tried it on. Perfect fit.

No big deal. He would have it back in the morning and cleaned before they opened. It wasn't the first time he had borrowed clothes from the cleaner. There was something almost irresistible about nice clothes. It was like he could become someone else, someone worthy.

As he set the coat aside, Chris felt something inside the pocket. He wondered what it was, but the buzzer for the drive-through sounded and he hurried to get one more load.

Finally Mr. Tomasi shooed him out. "Go on. Get home before it gets any worse."

Chris didn't really care. He had nothing to do tonight, or any night, for that matter. Mr. Tomasi went in the back, and Chris pulled on the coat and headed out into the snow.

The sidewalks were still crowded, and he could see people with grocery bags, probably buying all the milk and bread to stock up for the storm.

The temperature had dropped unexpectedly, and he was glad he had the peacoat. He pulled it tighter. It fit his long arms perfectly and looked good with his old jeans and worn sneakers. He ran his fingers through his curly brown hair to brush off the snowflakes, smoothed the front of the coat, then tucked his hands in the pockets for warmth.

There it was, the paper he had felt earlier. He paused under an awning in the entranceway of an office building. His fingers closed around the paper, and he pulled it out and opened it.

The Lord is my shepherd.

It was a Bible verse. He read the next line.

I shall not want.

That's when it came—the wanting, the ache inside. He rubbed his chest and took a deep breath. The ache was still there as he stood on the sidewalk in his borrowed coat, confused about the tears welling up in his eyes.

A long time ago in Hayville he had learned that it is safer not to want. If you didn't want, you couldn't be disappointed. It was the expectation of dinner that made you hungry . . . and mad when there was nothing to eat. It was the yearning to go to the movie that made you hurt when others had money for the ticket and you stayed home. It was the longing to be included in the party that made you disappointed when the invitation didn't come.

He rested back against the columns of the building and looked out at the city and the world and the people. Cars moving, honking. People hurrying. The world in motion. Chris felt like he alone was standing still, invisible and empty. He had thought that when he moved here, everything would change. His surroundings had changed, but he was the same inside. Empty.

What was it that he wanted? What did he ache for? Not to be invisible? Not to be empty? That was not likely to happen. Here in the city he was getting by. He could pay his rent and eat. That was incredible. But he still could not enjoy it. The want was still there. Looking out from the store windows around him stood a cast of mannequins, dressed in fine suits and silk dresses, but plastic, unfeeling.

He tucked the psalm into the inside pocket of the coat. It lay on his chest like a hand placed over his heart. The words stirred up feelings long ago suppressed.

Chris started down the sidewalk moving with the flow of people. A woman in a fur coat walked a Yorkie. A man in a double-breasted suit walked briskly past, holding a newspaper over his head to catch the wet snow. In the middle of all these people, Chris was alone.

He passed a large church. Stone steps led up to the dark wooden doors that were closed tight—offering no warmth against the chill outside. The verse in his pocket, however, was comforting, inviting.

"Are you up there, God?" he said to the gray sky.

No answer. There was no God in his world, and there hadn't been for a while.

"If you're there, God," he said, "it might be a good time to show me."

Still nothing. The doors of the church stayed closed. He shrugged and continued down the sidewalk toward home.

He smiled at the thought of God showing himself. When he was eight, a family across town had taken him to Sunday School. In the Bible stories he had heard, God was always appearing to people—once in a burning bush, another time in a pillar of fire. The family had eventually moved away, and he'd felt that wanting again—wanting to be back in Sunday School, to hear stories that made him hope for something more. Those stories seemed like fairy tales to him now. He pulled the jacket tighter against the cold. He felt the paper crinkle in the pocket.

Chris turned the corner to Market Street, which was crowded for a Friday evening. In the midst of the sea of dark-colored hats and scarves ahead of him, he caught sight of a spot of red. The red circle of color pulled him like a magnet as it bobbed up and down.

Chris stepped up his pace and watched the red circle. As he drew closer, he realized it was a hat, a red beret, and he could see that it was worn by a girl, a young woman, really. Her long brown hair hung out from beneath the beret, and her tweed jacket fit perfectly. Polyester/wool/acrylic he suspected—definitely "dry clean only." He strained not to lose her in the crowd.

The snow let up and changed to a drizzle. The evening was dreary, but Chris felt more alive as he pursued the red beret. Then, when he thought he had lost her, he stopped, almost brushing against her as she entered a building. He watched her glide through the glass doors, and he paused just long enough to read the sign outside—HOLY GROUNDS COFFEE SHOP.

A little corny. But, still, it looked peaceful and warm inside.

Chris went through the doors and at once noticed the aroma of freshly ground coffee. It was as if he had never experienced the smell before. The pitiful can of grocery brand coffee in his apartment had dulled his senses and left him out of touch with the real thing. He inhaled deeply and looked around the room.

There was a brightness and warmth and color that drew him in and made him breathe deeper. Signs above the counter had exotic names: Sumatra, Kona, Java, Mocha. Then there were specialty drinks like Love-Your-Neighbor Latte and Capernaum Cappuccino. There was a whole new vocabulary here.

He had walked home from the dry cleaner's every day for the last five months and had never noticed this place. How could all this have been going on without him?

He watched the girl in the red beret as she ordered. Her face was radiant and full of energy, her cheeks rosy with the blush of the cold evening air. She was all movement as he stood watching her. She shed her jacket and waved to a few friends.

He backed up against the wall, not ready to come in completely but not wanting to be left outside any longer. The chatter of voices and soft music playing beckoned him, but fear stopped him. Haunting voices of Hayville and rejection filled his mind.

As he watched, the barista placed a cup of coffee in her hand. She stood for a moment, pulling out her wallet to pay. As she passed the bills over, she glanced his way.

Then looked again. Then smiled. He watched her gather her change and drop it into the tip jar. She laughed with the girl behind the counter, then moved toward a table with her coffee.

His knees felt weak. She had smiled at him. He looked around to make sure it wasn't for another person. No, the smile was for him.

He watched as she settled alone at a small iron table. She leaned over her cup and breathed deeply, taking in the smell and steam rising from the cup. Chris stood like a zombie, the living dead.

He had read one time about moving from darkness into light. It was dangerous to move too quickly. The eye could only adjust so much to light. He thought it was the same thing with possibilities. There had been none in his life for so long that he had forgotten that choices existed.

He watched the girl rifle through her brown satchel. Her hair gleamed in the lamplight of the coffee shop. She pulled out a box of stationery and a pen. She sat staring off for a moment, then began to write.

It had been years since he'd had a real conversation with anyone besides Mr. Tomasi.

He practiced in his mind what he would say.

"Hello." *No, too formal.*

"Hi." *That was better.*

He had the opening word. But then what? It might be a mistake to say anything at all. Maybe he should leave. He glanced at the door. He felt that ache again and put his hand on his chest. There was the paper, still in the pocket.

He pulled it out and unfolded it. Mrs. McConnell's handwriting was sure and concise. The words were clear and had been written with such conviction that he could feel the imprint of the writing even on the back.

The Lord is my shepherd; I shall not want, he read. Each word had been printed neatly and carefully. She had believed the promise on the paper. Maybe he could, too.

He looked around at the people in the shop—some alone, others engrossed in a book or computer, some chatting in small groups or laughing and enjoying one another's company.

As he thought of the psalm, memories flooded him—memories of Sunday School and the simplicity of faith. The picture of Jesus carrying a lamb across his shoulders. He remembered the color and fun and an intensity of smells and tastes. Back then everything had been possible. He had loved God then for a season. When had he become so cynical? So alone?

He smelled the coffee and realized the waste that his life had become.

"I shall not want," he said.

There was that ache. Chris was suddenly overcome with wanting, and there was so much right in front of him. It was as if God was there, waiting for him to accept the richness of the world. Maybe he had been too hard on God. Maybe God was more than the dark, empty church he passed by every day.

He moved to the counter and was taken in by the bounty of pastries—apple-nut muffins, blueberry scones, chocolate-chip Danish. They were all color and texture, some covered with chocolate icing, others drizzled with glaze—a doughnut covered with red sprinkles. He felt like he had as a boy, pressing his nose up against the glass window of a toy store.

"I want . . ." he said. He thought of the hard-earned money in his pocket. He had more than enough for the week, but he was still afraid to spend it. Afraid there might not be more. Afraid of hunger. The fear of wanting made him live in want.

"Yes?" the girl behind the counter said, eyebrows raised.

There was too much choice. An abundance. He felt panic rising in his chest, and for a moment, he thought he might just leave.

"I shall not want," he said under his breath, almost like a battle cry. In his mind he held the image of the shepherd carrying the sheep and the kind expression of love on the shepherd's face. He wanted that love. He prayed for the first time in his adult life the simple prayer of a child. *Help me.*

The world opened, and light flooded in, bringing a million choices.

"Cappuccino." The word popped out, like he had said it all his life. "Cappuccino," he said again, just because it felt so good to make a choice. "Yes, I want a Capernaum Cappuccino."

He let out a sigh of relief. His shoulders relaxed, and though it seemed like such a small thing, he felt like he had just climbed Mount Everest.

The girl seemed relieved. "Okay. Anything else?"

He looked at the pastries. A chocolate Danish caught his attention; glistening sugar and deep rich chocolate pieces made his mouth water. "And a chocolate-chip Danish," he said, ignoring the price.

He was filled with warmth and felt as giddy as a child.

He waited for his order, watching the girl in the red beret.

"Her name's Pam," the girl behind the counter said as she handed him a steaming cup.

He blushed.

"I saw you looking."

He nodded.

"She likes the raspberry scones," the girl said with a smile.

Chris watched Pam stir her coffee.

Okay, God, he prayed for the second time, *let's go.*

He ordered again. "I'll take a raspberry scone."

He paid for his order and stood for a moment with the small bag of pastries and his steaming cup of coffee. He was drawn to the table, the red beret showing the way like a beacon. Past the other tables, across what felt like the longest room in the world, he walked until he came to her table and caught his breath.

"Hi," he said. "I'm Chris."

She stopped stirring her coffee and looked up at him. She had the bluest eyes he had ever seen. His heart skipped.

Then something amazing happened.

She smiled. This time it could only be for him.

"Hi," she answered. "Pam."

She pulled aside the satchel and offered him the empty seat beside her.

Chris put his things down and took off the coat. He smoothed his worn flannel shirt, unashamed, sat down beside her, and breathed deep, experiencing it all. The smells. The tastes. The sound of her voice.

He looked at the letter she was writing. *Dear Deke* was at the top of the page.

"Is that to your boyfriend?" Chris asked.

She shook her head no.

"My brother, Deke, is in Iraq. I'm sending him a letter."

Chris let out a sigh of relief. Brother—not boyfriend. He suddenly loved her brother!

She lifted her pen and looked at him, not like his customers who looked through him. He pulled the pastries out of the bag. They were rich and inviting: the warm golden scone with flecks of sugar, deep-red raspberry oozing from the side, and the plump Danish with slightly melted chocolate chips dotting the top.

"Have one."

"Thanks." Pam looked at the raspberry scone. "Julie must have told you what I like."

Chris nodded.

"I like to come here sometimes," she said. "My apartment gets lonely. You know what I mean?"

Chris nodded. He did.

He fingered the white paper in his hand.

"What's that?"

"Something I found." Chris thought of Mrs. McConnell and how pleased she would be to think of her Bible verses being given away. He wanted to give something to Pam. "You could send this to your brother."

Chris handed her the paper. There was a little coffee on the edge, but she didn't seem to notice. She opened it.

"Psalm 23. Cool. It's one of my favorites."

"I remember it from when I was little," Chris said.

"Me, too." She looked down at the paper. "It always makes me feel loved."

"Me, too," Chris said. And he realized it was true.

"So, I can send it to my brother?"

Chris nodded. He watched her fold the paper and put it into the pink envelope.

"Nice coat," she said, nodding to the borrowed peacoat.

"It's not mine," Chris said. He wanted to be Chris, not someone else. He wanted her to know him as he was.

Surrounded by sounds, smells, tastes, and the fullness of life, he was overwhelmed with God's love for him.

He remembered what he'd had said to God as he walked home earlier: "If you're there, it might be a good time to show me." He smiled when he thought of the burning bush and the pillar of fire. That probably would have scared him to death. For him, God had shown up with a red beret and a cup of coffee.

Soft light wrapped the table. The world seemed full of possibilities and hope. Chris felt a love and acceptance that had nothing to do with the pretty girl smiling at him from across the table. He was loved by God, a God who wanted him to have an abundant life.

Tomorrow he would be back at the dry cleaner's, invisible again to the customers, but not invisible to God. And he was no longer empty. Inside, a spark of hope, of new possibilities, was growing. The ache was gone.

Chris felt his world shifting like sand beneath his feet, just like one time when a school trip had taken him to the ocean. He hadn't thought of the ocean in years, but suddenly he could almost taste the salt air and hear the seabirds cry above him.

He prayed a prayer, his third in over a decade, but the best prayer that he could imagine. *Thank you, God.*

CHAPTER

three

---

*He makes me lie down
in green pastures*

---

*T*ELL ME what you remember, Private Johnson."

Dr. Mitchell sat down on the camp stool beside Deke Johnson's cot. Deke's large hands moved restlessly on his lap. His gray-green eyes were questioning and thoughtful. He knew he was in the medical unit and that he had been hurt in a mission.

"Nothing." Deke tried hard to remember, but his thoughts were confusing—like bits of paper blowing around in the tornado that was his mind. He could remember last week just fine, but the events of the past few days escaped him.

He lifted his hands palms up in a gesture of helplessness.

"Take your time."

Deke closed his eyes for a moment. A few scattered images came to mind.

"A clothesline . . . ," he said, "with a sheet."

"Good. Tell me about the sheet."

"It was white, crisp, snapping in the breeze. It reminded me . . ." Deke lapsed into silence. Some dark thought was lurking, coming closer.

"Go on. What did it remind you of?"

Deke moved his thoughts away from the darkness. He looked out the window of the hospital at the square of blue sky and blinked.

"My mother in Montana and Pam, my sister. My mother hated clothes dryers, and she always hung the sheets out on the clothesline in the backyard. Pam and I played in the middle of the sheets, like a fort or a hiding place."

The memory came to him like a dream. The sun through the aspen trees. The laughter of children as they ran carefree in the tall green grass and between the sheets. The sheets, clean and white on a line held by a cross of beams.

"The sun came through the sheets," Deke began. "Pam . . ."

He stopped and gazed out the window. The scene in his mind evaporated.

"Pam? Tell me about Pam."

"Pam's my little sister. She lives in Baltimore now. She's in nursing school. I just got a letter from her last week."

Deke closed his eyes, remembering. Mail call was the best time of the day. His friend Tater got his usual weekly letter from his parents. Tater would read the letter misty-eyed, complain of allergies, then stow the letter away under his bed. Deke had gotten Pam's letter in a pink envelope, and the guys had razzed him about it.

"Cool it, guys. It's from my sister."

"That's what they all say," Tater had said, blowing him a kiss.

He missed his friend. Where was Tater? Tater was the youngest in the unit, straight out of high school. A red-faced, sandy-haired combination of kid and soldier from

North Carolina, always touching the cross that he wore around his neck with his dog tag. Before each mission, Tater would kiss the cross. There was something innocent and trusting about that gesture.

Deke was afraid to ask about Tater. Something about the question was dangerous.

Deke thought about his letter from Pam and the paper inside—the twenty-third psalm.

"Pam sent me a psalm—the one about the green pastures. 'He makes me lie down in green pastures.'"

As many times as Deke had read the twenty-third psalm, he hadn't thought about that verse before. But Tater had. When Deke told Tater about the psalm, Tater recited the whole thing from memory.

Deke could remember Tater's comment. "He makes me lie down in *green* pastures—not tan like here—tan sand, tan fatigues, tan tents, tan everything!"

"Even the chow is tan," Deke had added.

Tater had laughed, then looked away. "Sometimes I close my eyes and pretend I'm not here—that I'm in a place, a green place, with cool breezes and tall grass blowing in the wind. But when I open my eyes, I'm still here."

"Tell me more about the psalm," the doctor said, breaking his thoughts. "Where is it now?"

"The psalm was in my pocket. I had it when . . ."

Dark thoughts came closer. Panic started rising.

"When . . ."

The small panic in his chest grew. Deke tried to remember more. He began to sweat. His hands increased their nervous movement.

"I don't remember what happened . . . I can't . . ."

"Take some deep breaths, Private."

"I can't!"

"Breathe! In and out. In and out."

Deke tried to breathe normally, but he gasped air in and exhaled erratically.

"No more!"

"Then let's take a break," the doctor said, calmly.

Deke lay back on the pillow and closed his eyes.

Dr. Mitchell closed his notebook and left silently.

"GOOD MORNING, Private Johnson."

"Hi, Doc." Deke looked up from his crossword puzzle.

Dr. Mitchell sat in his usual spot by the cot. In a soft voice he asked, "Is anything coming back?"

Deke hesitated. He put the puzzle book down and looked at the doctor. The doctor's kind eyes invited him to talk.

"I remember the morning of the patrol."

Deke's hands began to move rhythmically against the sheets.

"Tell me about it."

"It was early when we left—before dawn. A routine mounted security patrol. Tater and the others were griping, like always." Deke smiled at the memory of the constant complaining. "We had been on two or three patrols a day, every day, all month. I was exhausted and bleary-eyed from lack of sleep. The whole unit was."

"What happened?"

"We got a call about suspected insurgents in an apartment building in town."

The doctor waited, then said, "Go on."

"We parked the Strykers in front of the building. Tater and I dismounted, and Sergeant Donald motioned us inside to check it out. I remember walking into the apartment. I remember the room. Cockroaches everywhere. Dirty clothes on the floor. Food in the sink. The sour smell."

Deke's hands moved faster.

"I remember Tater kissing his cross, like he always did. Then we heard popping outside. Bullets hit the window, and glass shattered into the room. We hit the ground. We just lay there for a minute catching our breath. Tater kept kissing that stupid cross, like he wanted God to come and help us."

"Then what?"

"There were steps leading up to the roof. And blue sky at the top. I headed up the stairs slowly, watching every step. Tater was close behind me. We moved carefully, ready."

Deke stopped. There was something else—something hazy skirting around the edge of his mind. He took a sip of water but spilled some of it.

"I saw . . . ," Deke began.

"Take your time."

The dark thought, lurking so near, was too much for him, and he began to tremble uncontrollably.

"It's okay, Private."

The doctor stood and took Deke's hands.

"Calm down."

Deke's hands continued to shake.

"I'm right here, Private."

No answer.

"Nurse!"

A needle brought relief, and Deke drifted to sleep.

———

DR. MITCHELL SAT DOWN on the small camp stool and balanced his notebook on his knee. "Good morning."

Deke turned away. "I don't want to talk about the mission."

The day before had brought troubling thoughts, and the night had been filled with nightmares, dark images chasing him, nearer and nearer.

"No need to."

Deke turned back and looked at the doctor.

"We can talk about something else. You mentioned a piece of paper, a psalm?"

The memory of the psalm brought Deke peace and courage. He could talk about the psalm. "Yeah, I got a letter from my sister. She was mad 'cause I hadn't answered her emails."

"Why didn't you?"

"Nothing new to say. And it was too hard to pretend."

"Pretend?"

"Yeah, pretend that this was some kind of vacation or something. You know, people are dying over here."

"Like who?"

"Like John Henderson, Juan Golendez, Pete Mancini, like all the guys I came over with. Do we have to talk about that?"

"No."

"Good."

"What about the paper that your sister sent? You've mentioned it twice."

"Yeah, she sent me Psalm 23. The Lord is my shepherd. You know it?"

"Yes."

"The lying down in green pastures part made me remember Montana."

"Is your mother still in Montana?"

"Yeah, she's still in the farmhouse where we grew up."

"The house with the clothesline?"

"I don't want to talk about the clothesline."

"Tell me about the sheet."

Darkness moved closer to Deke. "What sheet?"

"You said you remembered a sheet? A white sheet . . . snapping?"

Deke fought the thoughts moving closer.

"That's all," he said. "I'm sorry, Doc. That's all I can do now."

The thoughts in Deke's mind still blew in a whirlwind of a dark vortex, yet glimmers of light seemed to begin to penetrate the darkness. Darkness and light. Green pastures and tan desert. A tug-of-war in contrasts.

"That's fine. We'll talk again."

When Dr. Mitchell left, Deke thought about the mission. Bits and pieces floated in his mind like the pieces of a puzzle. Some were falling into place. There was the roof. And yelling. And Tater. Something about Tater. Other pieces of the puzzle were still missing, and some pieces weren't turned over yet.

Deke just wanted some peace in his mind. He was confused and exhausted. He kept coming back to the psalm on the paper and the idea of lying down. Here he was flat on his back, yet he couldn't rest. The image of Tater kissing the cross kept coming to mind. Tater got great comfort from that cross. Tater's faith gave him peace.

Deke looked at Dr. Mitchell's empty stool and imagined Jesus sitting there. The look on the face of Jesus was not one of condemnation, but of great love and compassion. Only Jesus could end this torture.

Jesus, take me out of the hell that my mind has become. Help me lie down in green pastures.

Deke gave it to God—the memories, the injury, the lying down, the mess of his mind. Peace descended. Thoughts still jumbled in his head, but he was no longer anxious about them. Jesus was near. Whatever came, Deke would embrace it with God.

He closed his eyes. Slowly, seeping into his consciousness, the memories came into focus.

"GOOD MORNING, Private Johnson."

"Good morning, Doc."

Deke was sitting on the edge of his cot, leaning forward. His hands rested in a relaxed way on his knees.

45

"You look different," the doctor said.

"I remember. I remember it all." It was a relief to say it. The words were bursting to be released.

"Do you want to tell me?"

Deke hesitated, but thought of Tater's faith and Jesus. "Yes. I saw . . ."

He faltered, fear rising.

"You can do this, Private." The doctor paused, then said softly, "What did you see?"

"We were at that apartment where the insurgents were supposed to be. I was the point man going up the stairs to the roof. Then Tater. Then the others. I moved toward the opening, then stepped up onto the roof. I saw . . ."

"Go on."

"I saw a clothesline, stretched across the rooftop, with white sheets hanging, blowing in the breeze. The sun was coming through, and there was a shadow behind the sheet. Hiding, someone hiding. I raised my weapon."

"Yes?"

"I froze, Doc. I remembered home. I remembered Pam, hiding in the sheets on the clothesline, and I couldn't shoot. I couldn't. I didn't know."

"No, you couldn't know."

"Someone was back there—in the shadows."

"You saw shadows."

"Then the sheet snapped. No. The noise, the snapping, it wasn't the sheet. It was . . ."

The dark in his mind was moving closer, but this time Deke turned to face it.

"A weapon. The noise, it was rounds going by my head. An insurgent hiding behind the sheet was firing at us. I was hit and down. The man kept firing. Tater fell to the ground beside me. I saw blood . . ."

"Go on."

Light flooded Deke's mind.

"Then the guy jumped off the roof and got away. Everything was silent."

"What happened next?"

"'Tater. Tater!' I called, but no answer. There was so much blood. There was blue sky. No green. Then there was chaos all around me as others arrived to help."

Deke was breathing hard. He caught his breath and made himself calm down. He folded his hands in his lap. They were not shaking.

"I couldn't shoot," he said, throwing his arms up in a gesture of surrender. "I couldn't shoot."

The image of the sheets in Montana and Pam and the other children running through, casting shadows, came to his mind.

"I didn't know."

Deke paused and took a deep breath.

"We were wounded, both of us. Tater and me. There, lying on the roof, with my knee blown apart, I pulled out the paper."

"The psalm?"

"Yes, I read it to him, to Tater. 'The Lord is my shepherd.' Tater's lips moved as I read the words. He knew them by heart."

"Then?"

"When we got to the part about the green pastures . . . 'He makes me lie down in green pastures' . . ."

"Go on."

"He let go. Tater let go."

Tears flowed freely down Deke's face. Good tears, cleansing tears, tears releasing his friend. As Deke wept, the doctor sat still beside him.

"He just let go," Deke said, softly.

Time stopped, and the two men sat together as the thoughts and words settled around them.

"Do you think he would forgive me?" Deke asked.

"Who?"

"Tater."

"For what?"

"For not shooting."

"What do you think?"

Deke sat motionless, thinking of Tater's peaceful face as Deke read the psalm.

"Yes."

Deke sighed. The darkness in his mind dissipated. The light from the small window cast a square of light on the cot.

"Yes," he repeated. His body relaxed.

They sat for a moment staring at the square of light.

"Do you still have the psalm?"

"No. As the helicopter medevac'd us out of there, the psalm blew out of my hand. The last I saw of it, the paper was blowing across the desert like a white flag."

"What an image, a white flag."

Deke was breathing easily now.

"What do think about the psalm?" he asked. "Do you think Jesus sent it to me?"

"What do you think?"

"I think He did—to remind me that He is with me."

"That makes sense to me."

"And to give Tater peace. At the end."

"Yes."

Deke felt the warmth of the sun coming in from the window, and his thinking was clear.

"Are you ready to go home now?"

"Yes, Doc. I think I can rest now."

"Well, you're scheduled for surgery stateside, then rehab, so there'll be plenty of time for lying down," Dr. Mitchell said.

"I think he's lying down, too," Deke said.

"Who?"

"Tater."

Deke eyes filled with tears as he remembered Tater's lips moving along with the words of the psalm.

"Tater's home," Deke said. "I think Tater's home."

The doctor left, and Deke was alone. He thought about Tater and the good times they'd had together. His friend laughing. Kissing his cross. Guarding the pile of letters from his parents.

Deke imagined Tater in a place, a green place, with cool breezes and tall grasses blowing in the wind.

He imagined Tater in heaven looking down at him, smiling.

CHAPTER

Four

He leads me beside still waters

THE HABOOB CAME UPON THEM suddenly as they drove on the highway toward their new lives in Turkey. Clouds of dry, stinging sand rolled across the desert, obscuring their vision and halting their progress to an uncertain future as war refugees.

Nadia did not notice the storm moving toward their small car. She was distracted by her older sister, who would not share her paper. Sevin never shared, but that didn't stop Nadia from trying.

"Please, Sevin. Just one piece of paper?"

Sevin did not even look over. "No!"

"Please?"

"No."

"I need paper, too," Nadia's little brother, Aza, chimed in. "I want to send a letter."

"No!"

They were all tired and hot and out of patience. They had been in the car for hours, and time passed slowly. The backseat was tightly packed. Around them was everything they owned at this moment, which was everything they could fit into the small car. Father was behind the wheel, his attention focused on the road ahead. Beside him, Mother saw the storm first.

"Haboob," she said, pointing at the brown billowing clouds on the ground moving toward them. She sat up and leaned forward, her eyes looking intently, brow wrinkling into worry.

Father looked concerned but did not stop driving.

Without a word they began rolling up the car windows, then tightening their scarves, zipping bags closed, and covering their mouths to protect from the sand and grit that was approaching.

Sevin pulled Aza's scarf over his head and snuggled his head down onto her lap. Nadia watched the storm move closer as they kept driving toward the border. It seemed to chase them across the desert.

"It's coming so fast," she said. "Can we outrun it?"

Father glanced at the wall of sand, now almost upon them. He shook his head. Mother reached around to tuck the scarf tighter around Aza, then turned back to the front seat and pulled her own scarf over her mouth.

The first bits of grit began to hit the windows, and Father pulled the car to the side of the road. The motor stopped, and in the silence they heard the whistle of the wind and the tiny grains of sand pelting the windows. Father took a deep breath, then covered his own mouth. He sat still, his head leaning back on the headrest. The car rocked with the gusts of wind. They waited.

Outside, all disappeared in a sea of dismal brown. The whir of the wind increased to a roar around the small Honda. The dust and grit seeped through unseen cracks, and Nadia closed her eyes against the nothingness. Her mouth was dry and she wanted a drink, but she knew there was too little water and she did not ask.

Always, the problem was water. At first they could get

water only every other day. Mother would fill the buckets and tubs, and they would make the water last until the next day. Then the water stopped altogether. Then they had to carry water from the central well, and the line was long. Sometimes Father had to wait overnight, or longer.

The war had left them without water, but mainly without safety and peace. So now they were leaving their country.

The wind grew louder, and tiny pebbles hit the car. In the midst of the sand and pebbles, a paper smacked against the windshield. It remained glued in place by the wind.

Paper, Nadia thought. *A piece of paper for me!*

She stared at it, silently claiming it as her own. Suddenly, between gusts, it fell to the ground, out of sight. Quickly, Nadia pressed her face against the glass, looking left and right, trying to spot the paper. She craned her neck up and down, but it was useless in the sea of brown. Finally she gave up and huddled with the rest of the family as they waited anxiously for the storm to pass.

Smack! The paper hit the car again, this time from the other side, blown back by the swirling wind.

"Paper," she said, her voice lost in the roar of the wind.

The wind slowly inched the paper across the window to the edge. The paper seemed to be holding on by a thread. Then, whoosh, it was gone again.

So close. She waited for it to come back, but there was no sign of it in the whirling grit.

The day before they left, Nadia had gone with her father

to the bird market. The sound alone was amazing: the cries, caws, shrieks, chirps, and trills of the different birds. Thousands upon thousands of birds—cages and cages, stacked from floor to ceiling. In one cage alone there were more than a hundred wrens, a mass movement of flapping wings and restless shifting. Two turkeys sat alone in a wooden cage, gobbling back and forth. Owls, brightly colored parrots, gray cockatiels, and so many others—stuck in cages.

Nadia felt stuck, too—almost invisible. As the oldest, Sevin was able to go to school, even to learn English, and Sevin was able to work in the salon after classes. Aza was the youngest and the boy. The world seemed to revolve around him. Nadia was just in the middle, stuck like the birds—caged, restless, waiting.

She felt trapped—trapped by everything around her. Her life was missing something, and she was restless to find it. Whatever was missing, she knew she would have to learn it on her own. Nadia felt that way now in their small car: waiting, restless for the time when she could get out and look for her paper. Somehow she felt that the paper was hers. Unfortunately, it was probably long gone, but as soon as the storm was over, she planned to check anyway.

When the storm finally passed, they opened the car doors to brush away the piles of sand. Aza emerged from his scarf, his eyelashes and brows dusted with sand. Father's mustache was covered with the fine powder.

Nadia jumped out of the car and shook off her scarf and brushed off her clothes. She slipped her feet out of her plastic shoes and ran around the car. That's when she saw the paper, caught by the tire. She picked it up and shook it off, then flattened it out on her arm. The words were in a foreign language, maybe English from the soldiers.

She watched while Father filled the radiator with water. She tried not to think about the water being poured into the car. Her tongue was dry with thirst. She studied her paper. She wished she could read it. It was nice paper, white and thick, not like the thin brown paper that Sevin used for school. The words were written in a strong handwriting in bright blue ink. Maybe by a woman, a strong woman.

"Sevin." Nadia tugged her sister's sleeve. "I think my paper is English. Will you read it for me?"

Her sister was busy shaking out her clothes and adjusting her scarf. She brushed the dust off her face and hair.

"No!"

"Please?"

"No."

"Read for her," Mother said. She leaned over the front of the car, watching Father fill the radiator. Mother dabbed the beads of sweat on the side of her face and began organizing the bags, shaking off the sand and repositioning them in the car. Every spare inch of the car was full.

Sevin took the paper and looked at it. She shook it out, then held it up as if it were way too much trouble to read the simple words. Finally she lowered it, looked down at the paper, and studied the words.

"It is about God," she said. "The Christian God."

"Huh?" said Father, looking up from the engine. "What is there to say?"

"Is it about war?" Aza asked. He danced around Sevin. "Is it about God defeating the enemies?"

"No."

Nadia held her breath and remained silent. If she showed how badly she wanted something, Sevin might refuse her.

Sevin frowned as she made out the words. "It says he is a . . ."

"What?"

"Quiet," she said. "I'm translating."

Without moving or taking a breath, Nadia watched Sevin. For some reason Nadia couldn't quite grasp, she wanted desperately to know the words written on the paper by the strong woman.

Sevin cleared her throat.

"It says he is a shepherd."

She thrust the paper back at Nadia and exclaimed, "What kind of warrior would a shepherd make? What kind of a god is that?!"

"Yes," Mother said. "Can you imagine such a thing? A god who is a lowly shepherd."

They all laughed.

"No weapons?" Aza asked. He kicked the small stones beside the car.

"No," Sevin said. "Just sheep."

"Dirty sheep," Father added.

This brought on another round of laughter as they loaded back into the car. They crawled in among the bundles and settled back into their places. Father started the engine, and puffs of fine dust blew out of the vents as the car began to move.

"A god who is a shepherd," Nadia said, letting the idea settle in her mind. It wasn't so funny to her. It was exciting. She sat back and thought.

At home they had often heard the bombs whizzing overhead, and she'd wondered what would happen if she died. Had she been good enough? Would Allah punish her? She knew her father and mother had the same fear of Allah.

What if God was a shepherd? She knew about shepherds; they took care of their sheep, even stinky ones. The sheep were not afraid of the shepherd. They loved the shepherd and felt safe with him. She would like to feel safe and loved.

Nadia thought about her life. Everything was changing. Everything was uncertain. The little love and security in her life came in dribbles, like water. What would it be like to have a shepherd God watching over her—a shepherd God who loved her and cared for her—a life of love and security, not fear? Behind her was a dry, barren existence—ahead, she felt, was life.

Aza leaned close, touching the paper gently. "I want the paper, too. I want to send a letter to Jwan." He already missed his best friend, Jwan, from home.

Nadia looked nervously to the front seat, waiting for Mother to make her give the paper to Aza. A small snore came from her mother, and Nadia breathed relief.

"We can't send a letter yet," Nadia said. "We have to wait until we get to Adana."

He seemed satisfied.

She stared at the words on her paper. She wanted to ask Sevin to read it to her again, but her sister was sitting with her head resting back, eyes closed.

Nadia ran her finger over the words. Then suddenly she saw one word that she recognized: *water!*

She smiled. The paper said *water.* She knew that word from the bottles of water that the soldiers gave them. The paper was about the shepherd God and also about water.

"Sevin," she tugged her sister's arm.

Sevin did not open her eyes but pursed her lips in a pout.

"Just one more line. Please?" She pushed the paper into her sister's hand. "Just read to me about the water."

Nadia's mouth was dry as she handed Sevin the paper, and she felt more thirsty than ever. Sevin looked at the line and sighed.

"He leads me beside still waters," she read.

She gave the paper back. "That's all for now."

Nadia leaned her head against the window. The words were beautiful.

He leads me beside still waters. This was about the shepherd God who would lead his sheep to water. Could this God bring her family to water? Could he care for them like a shepherd cares for his sheep?

Across the desert she could see a camel caravan walking in the distance. The men who cared for the camels were always planning for the next source of water. A shepherd took care that his sheep had water, too. Without it they would die.

Shepherd God, she said in her mind, *If you are my shepherd, give me this water.*

In the middle of the crowded backseat Nadia felt peace, and she closed her eyes. For the first time in several days, she slept. As she slept, she dreamed of sheep being loved by a shepherd. The sheep did not do anything. The shepherd loved and cared for them, just as they were.

In her dream one of the sheep came closer and closer. She tried desperately to see the sheep's face but could not. The sheep kept circling the shepherd, with its face always just out of sight. At last the sheep turned abruptly, and she knew it was herself.

Nadia woke and thought about this shepherd God, who did not require her to be anything but a sheep of His.

As night fell, they arrived at the border. Sevin and Aza slept in the backseat as the family waited in the long lines to have their papers checked. Finally, when it was their turn, the men took a look at Father's documents and waved them into their new life.

It seemed that they were leaving behind the horror of war, along with the thirst and fear. Nadia held the paper closely as they drove on through the night. The hum of the tires was peaceful. The crowded backseat was comforting.

Dawn broke. They rounded the last bend of the mountain, and there it was. The sea! It stretched out in front of them. White dots of waves capped the surface— so blue and so clean. Best of all, there was so much. More water than she had ever seen—more than she even imagined. Could God be like that, so much more than anyone could imagine?

Aza was bouncing up and down on the car seat.

"Look at the boat!" he yelled.

A big green sailboat was anchored just offshore. A small dinghy from the sailboat was making its way to shore.

Father pulled the car over, and they piled out, running to the water. Mother laughed, a sound Nadia had not heard in years. The joy was overwhelming, the coolness of the water refreshing, the blueness soothing.

They played and laughed, then sat on the rocks.

Father took out the basket of food, and Nadia pulled the paper out again.

"Father, it's true," she said.

"What's true?"

"The paper says, 'He leads me beside still waters,' and here we are."

"Huh?" he said, not really listening.

Nadia leaned back and said, "I think God is big, big as the sea. Best of all, He cares for all of us, even me."

They drank fresh water from a public well by the picnic area. There was more than enough for everyone.

Nadia set the paper down beside her and closed her eyes. The sun warmed her face. Aza played, and the family dozed as the breezes blew over them.

Suddenly Aza came running up.

"Nadia, I sent it!" he yelled.

"What?"

"I sent Jwan a letter."

"What letter?"

"The one from the haboob."

Nadia looked at the empty sand beside her. Her paper was gone. Aza must have taken it.

"Who did you give it to?"

"The man on the boat, the big boat."

Out on the sea they could see the green sailboat moving away in the distance, the small dinghy trailing behind.

Nadia should have been angry, but there was no anger in her. The paper had blown into her life, teaching her about God, and she knew it was true. The god written about on this paper was the real God. He was a shepherd, who loved His sheep and cared for them and gave them water. She wanted to know more about this God. She would keep asking until she found someone to tell her more. She was thirsty again, but in a different way.

"Aza," she said, "look at the birds."

Above them the gulls hovered in the breeze. Unlike the captive birds in the cages at the town market, these birds were free, flying high in the blueness of the sky, flying high beside the still water.

Nadia's heart soared, and she felt as free as the birds.

CHAPTER

Five

He restores my soul

FRANÇOIS GINGERLY REMOVED the old painting from its cocoon of paper while the woman looked on anxiously.

"It was in my father's attic," she said. "I believe it's been there for almost a century."

"I see."

François turned the painting over. Years of restoration work had taught him to look at the back first. He could tell much more from the back.

The painting was on linen, very brittle, with a medium-sized tear near the top. He gently ran his fingers along the inside edge—not bad for a hundred-plus years old, but it would definitely require some careful work.

He turned it back over.

"The chimney leaked into the attic," she said apologetically. "So there's some dirt on the painting."

That was an understatement. This was one of the dirtiest pieces of art François had ever seen, and he'd seen quite a few in his forty years in the restoration business. There was so much grime and soot on this painting that it was difficult to make out the figures in the scene. Who knew what else might be on the canvas?

François was always hopeful. He remembered an Italian painting of the prodigal son that a colleague had cleaned, only to discover that the son was arriving home in a boat. The boat had been completely hidden by the buildup of centuries of dirt and dust.

"I don't know if I should have it restored," she said hesitantly.

It was the question measured by everyone who entered his shop. Was the painting valuable enough to restore? Was it worth the money and time and energy? François asked himself the same question.

"I can clean it first," he offered, "then you can decide whether you'd like further work."

"So, what is the price for cleaning?"

"Three hundred euro."

The woman stared at the painting.

"It was my grandfather's. He might have even painted it himself . . ." She paused.

François was usually the one to waver at this point and drop the price, but his wife had always encouraged him to stand firm. "You are valuable, and people either value your service or they do not," she'd said. Now that she was gone, he was even more resolved to follow her advice.

The woman let out a sigh. "All right. Go ahead."

She pulled out her wallet and paid the down payment.

When the woman left, François went back to his computer. His screen saver, William Dyce's painting *The Good Shepherd*, was bouncing around. He hit the space bar, and the entire painting filled the screen.

It had been his screen saver for six months and two days. He knew the exact date, because it was the day his wife, Annette, had died. A copy of the painting had hung in the room where she'd had her chemotherapy treatments, and she had taken to it immediately.

"Look, *chéri*," Annette had said, "how gently the shepherd carries the lamb." Her eyes had looked at the painting as if she was looking through a window. "Maybe He will carry me that way . . . when I go."

"No," François protested. "You are not going anywhere. You are staying right here with me."

Over the past six months and two days François had looked at the painting many times. Once again he studied the sheep with all the various shades of beige and brown and all the whites. He eyed the soft tenné colors of the robe that the shepherd was wearing, and that splash of blue. The colors were just right. He'd love to see the painting in person for a better look, but the original was in the Manchester Art Gallery and he was in Paris. So for now, the computer would have to do. It was hard to imagine going to see the painting without Annette.

The bell jingled, signaling another customer entering the shop. Two in one day—that was a lot. François hurried to the front. Visitors meant company, and he hadn't had much. The woman today was the first in two weeks.

"François, my friend. I've come to admire your latest project, whatever it may be."

It was Gérard, a friend of many years.

"Ah, the world traveler returns!" François realized that today he had spoken more words than in the previous two weeks combined.

Since Annette's death, there were a number of days when he spoke to no one. Slowly he had felt himself slipping from life; slowly his soul was waning away, like a fading moon.

"Gérard, my friend. Come and sit. I want to hear all about your sailing trip. Can I bring you coffee?"

"Yes, and make it strong. I will need strength."

François poured the coffee and added the touch of cream that he knew Gérard liked.

"My friend, why do you need strength?"

"Today I book my ticket on the Chunnel." He was going through his wallet and counting his cash.

"The Chunnel? You, Gérard Chantier, are going to ride the Chunnel?"

"Yes, all thirty-one miles of it. I will be two hundred and fifty feet below the surface of the water," he said with a shudder. "You know me. I like to be on top of the water!"

"Why not take a boat?"

"Too slow. Besides, they won't let me be captain!"

They both laughed.

"So, you are off to London," François said, trying not to show his disappointment.

When Gérard left town, François would likely see no one the entire time he was gone, save for an occasional customer. Lately François had wondered, if he died in his apartment, would it be weeks before anyone found his body?

"Yes, I'm off to London. And I hope this time while I'm gone you'll be back at the café. The boys tell me they did not see you once while I was gone sailing. Everyone misses you."

"I was busy," François lied. He hadn't felt much like being with his friends. He still felt empty inside, like a hollow piece of chocolate with a shell that looked good but no rich chocolate inside, just nothing.

"Ah, I almost forgot." Gérard pulled a piece of folded paper from the bills in his wallet. "Here. A little boy gave this to me when we stopped in Turkey."

François took the paper.

"It reminded me of you and that painting you like so much."

Gérard pointed to the image of *The Good Shepherd*, again bouncing back and forth on François's computer screen.

François didn't mention how the painting reminded him of his dear Annette.

When she had finally been admitted to the hospice wing of the hospital, the nurses had moved the picture into her room beside her bed. François had sat beside her day after day, hoping and praying for a miracle.

"Look, *chérie*," she had said one day, "how Jesus is carrying the lamb through the gate. Will you let me go? Can I go through the gate?"

"No," François had begged. "Don't leave me. You will get better. We will go to England and see this painting together."

Gérard interrupted his thoughts. "You could visit the painting, you know—if you went with me on the Chunnel."

"Oh, no." François held up his hands in protest. "I'm not going on that thing."

"Well," Gérard said, "we'll discuss it another day. Now I want to see your latest project."

"Aaaaaaaaaaah," François teased. "Something new came in today."

The men made their way to the restoration area in the back.

The large room consisted mostly of an old wooden table covered with bottles of chemicals: acetone, alcohol, linseed oil, turpentine, mineral spirits, and bowls of swabs and cotton balls.

The woman's dirty painting lay at one end of the table. Gérard hovered over it.

"Where'd this come from—the coal bin?"

François laughed.

"Aaaah, but what lies beneath?" Gérard said mysteriously.

"That is always the question," François said. "And who was the artist?"

Gérard clasped his hands in childlike excitement. "Yes, yes. Perhaps this one will be a great discovery for you. A famous artist—French, of course."

"Of course." François smiled.

He picked up a soft-bristle brush and began to gently dust the painting. When he finished, he picked up a cotton ball and dipped it in the cleansing gel. He started at the edge of the painting and dabbed carefully. The cotton ball came away covered in black.

Gérard watched intently, not speaking but breathing heavily. François repeated the procedure several times, and slowly a patch of green appeared.

"Maybe a pastoral scene," François said. He looked closely. It was painted with a thick flat surface that looked vaguely familiar. It was a style he recognized, but he couldn't remember where.

"I will return tomorrow to see the progress," Gérard said. "Right now, I'm off to get my Chunnel ticket."

When Gérard left, François pulled out the paper Gérard had gotten in Turkey. His English was pretty good, so he had no trouble reading it.

Psalm 23: The Shepherd's Song. He looked at the picture on his screen, and the final memory flooded back.

The last day the nurse had spoken to him in the hall with great kindness. "You have to let her go. She's hurting. She's hanging on because of you. You must tell her that she can go."

François had struggled with his thoughts, but he knew the nurse was right. For Annette's sake, he had to let her go.

As he came into the room, Annette smiled weakly. He sat beside her and held her hand for the last time. They looked at the picture together.

"Look," François said through his tears. "The shepherd is ready to take his sheep."

Annette nodded, looking at him with love.

"May . . . I . . . go?" She strained for each word.

"Go, my darling. Go through the gate with Jesus."

Six months of unshed tears came as François gripped the paper. Tears for Annette at first and the years that she would miss, then tears for himself and the love that he had lost that day.

He held the paper and read. *The Lord is my shepherd. I shall not want . . .* He continued down the page until he came to a phrase that stopped him.

He restores my soul.

That's what I need, François thought. *I need my soul restored.*

Lately he'd felt his soul was dead, but maybe it wasn't completely dead. He didn't know for sure. One thing he *did* know—before Annette's cancer, life had been brighter, clearer. Music had been sweeter. Now everything seemed dull and dark and flat. He looked at the grime on the painting and the small patch he had cleaned, now colorful and clear. Maybe his soul was just covered in grime—the grime of grief. Grime was oily and stuck hard to paintings; perhaps grief stuck hard to the soul.

François rubbed his chin. "But how in the world do you restore a soul?" He imagined a giant hand dabbing grime off his soul and a small bit of color appearing. *Oh, if it was only that easy,* he thought. *Besides, I am an old man. Who would restore the soul of an old man? There is no value there.*

François tossed the paper aside and picked up another cotton ball. He worked for a solid six hours, stopping only for small breaks. As he worked, it became increasingly clear that this was a painting of great quality. He dreamed of a Picasso, or Matisse, or Renoir, or Cézanne, but it was only a dream, certainly not a possibility.

As he worked, he thought about *The Good Shepherd* painting by Dyce. Jesus was the shepherd in that painting. He was holding a young lamb in his arms while the other sheep followed. A shepherd provided everything that his sheep needed—water, food, safety. What did François need? His wife! Who was he kidding? Nothing could replace his precious Annette.

"I wish it were easy," he said to the painting. "I wish a swab and a little cleaner could fix me."

He stood back and admired his work. Now half the meadow was in plain view, and the landscape was covered with red poppies. François's heart beat faster. This was quality work. The design, color, tone—all the work of a master. He grabbed another cotton ball. Next, he would finish the characters in the scene, then the artist's signature. He had been saving that for last.

No! He didn't want to wait. He would immediately turn his attention to the artist's signature. That's what he had wanted to do for the last couple of hours, but he had held back, enjoying the idea of possible greatness in front of him and not wanting to find out the truth, which was probably that the lady's grandfather was the artist and not one of the masters.

As François worked, his thoughts drifted once again to his soul. If it were going to be restored, it would have to be Jesus restoring it. François couldn't do it himself. He had tried to talk himself out of his depression for weeks now, and it wasn't working.

François looked at the wrinkles on his hands. He was old, no doubt about it, and maybe not worth restoring. Isn't that what you had to decide before you started a new restoration project? Was it worth it?

François glanced at the Dyce painting. Weren't all the

lambs valuable to Jesus? He thought he recalled a story in the Bible of a shepherd searching for one missing lamb even when he had ninety-nine others. A small ray of hope began to build inside François.

So, he thought as he worked, *if Jesus was going to restore my soul, how would He do it? He certainly doesn't have a big table with jars of cleaner.*

François thought about his own restoration work. The painting itself didn't know how it would be restored. It just was. And François didn't have to know how he would be restored. He just needed to believe that it would happen.

He stopped working and looked up at the ceiling. For a moment he stared at the cracks. He opened his mouth but could not speak. Then the tears came.

"Jesus," he whispered through his tears. "Jesus, please restore my soul."

He looked down at his painting; his tears were splattered across the signature. He wiped them away, then started to remove the final layer of grime with gentle strokes. As he did, letters appeared. First *P.* then *C* and *e* and *z.*

François stopped midstroke. He held his breath. Could it be? Surely not. He grabbed another cotton ball and worked gently: *a, n, n,* and finally *e.*

P. Cezanne. Paul Cézanne!

It made sense now. The thick, flat surface of paint. The repetitive, sensitive strokes that Cézanne was known for. The mastery of design, color, tone, composition, draftsmanship. It was so obvious now. And the poppies . . . Cézanne had lived in Aix-en-Provence, where the poppy fields were vibrant and beautiful.

François worked through the night finishing the cleaning, and in the early morning he fell asleep at his desk with *The Good Shepherd* circling on the computer screen at his head.

Banging on the shop door woke François at mid-morning. It was Gérard.

He clasped his hands together. "I have a surprise."

"I, too, have a surprise," François said. "But you first, my friend."

"I bought two!" Gérard announced excitedly.

"Two what?"

"Two tickets for the Chunnel." He pulled them out of his pocket and began waving them around and doing a little jig. "Now you must go with me to London, to London, to London."

François felt excitement rising in his chest, like when he and Annette were leaving for holiday. Yesterday the idea of going with Gérard seemed out of the question, impossible, crazy—but now the idea seemed so right.

This is a gift from God, François thought. *One step in restoring my soul.*

Suddenly his mind was racing with all the famous art in London. He could visit the National Gallery, the Tate Modern, and Somerset House, the Royal Academy of Arts, and the National Portrait Gallery. And the Wallace Collection. So much.

Gérard suddenly stopped dancing. "You will go, won't you?"

"Of course!" François joined Gérard in his jig.

"And Manchester is just a short train ride from London," Gérard sang. "From London, from London."

François would finally see *The Good Shepherd* in person.

Gérard stopped dancing. "What of your surprise?"

"Oh, come and see, my friend, come and see. You will not believe it."

Gérard followed François back to the restoration room where the Cézanne sat in all its restored beauty on an easel. From a distance Gérard immediately spotted the quality of the art, and he approached the painting slowly. With his hands clasped behind his back, he examined it closely, looking first at the signature, then at the painting itself, studying the strokes and color and turning his head in every possible angle.

Finally he spoke. "Magnificent!"

François beamed. "Indeed."

"This calls for a celebration," Gérard said, opening the cabinet door where François kept his wine. He pulled out two glasses and a bottle of Bordeaux. They poured the wine and pulled two chairs up in front of the Cézanne.

"To beautiful art!" Gérard said.

François lifted his glass.

"To Cézanne," François said.

Gérard lifted his glass.

They sat in their chairs, sipping wine and enjoying the painting.

"They say that a painting is never the same after restoration. That you can never completely take it back to what it was in the beginning when it was new. But I have always thought that the cracks and lines add beauty to the work. It becomes part of the character of the piece," mused François.

Gérard lifted his glass. "Well said."

François thought it was true for himself, too. Time and circumstances did their work, and the results were different from the original. Just like the painting, he was different now, and he would never be the same as he was before he lost Annette. He didn't even want to be the same. He had never experienced love as deeply as he had while helping her through her illness.

He glanced back over his shoulder at *The Good Shepherd* bouncing around his computer screen. There were some sheep that were already inside the gate, and there were some behind the shepherd, following but not yet inside. Perhaps that's how it was with him and Annette. She was already ahead of him inside the gate, and he was still outside. But someday the shepherd would carry him through the gate, too, and he would be with her again.

François looked at the sheep inside the fenced area, comfortably grazing. The line from the psalm came to him again: *He restores my soul.*

"To restoration," François said.

And they lifted their glasses in a grand toast.

CHAPTER

Six

He leads me in paths of righteousness
for his name's sake

---

*S*TOP! Stop that man!"

Patrick ran hard down the London street, not looking back. He didn't have to. He knew what was behind him. The police. They had seen him lifting the wallet from the old man at the train station.

Patrick didn't stop. He ran as fast as he could. His heart pounded, and he could feel sweat dripping from his forehead. His breath was ragged. Once you started running, it was hard to stop. He had been running for more than a year. His past was catching up to him, just like the policemen who were closing in.

He crossed the street, dodged a couple of cars, and ducked down an alley. He easily hurdled over a small fence and came out on the next street, where he paused for a moment, listening, waiting, heart pounding. His arms and legs were still strong from the days of running in the hills of Ireland, hurdling stone walls and running down the paths in the pasture. This was different.

He heard them coming. The police had guessed his move and were rounding the corner.

"Hey, you! Stop!"

Drat. They were way too close for comfort. He ran harder.

People jumped back from him on the sidewalk. Patrick formed a quick plan. It wasn't likely to work, but it was his only hope. If the café coming up ahead was crowded enough, then he could artfully dodge the customers and slip inside, through the kitchen, and out the back where his hotel had a back entrance.

Patrick rounded the corner. Good, it *was* crowded. That would slow down the police. He heard them behind him.

"Stop that man!"

Patrick darted between the tables and into the café. Out the back and a quick left. He entered the cheap hotel by the back door and took the stairs two at a time. He quickly ran into his room, slammed the door shut, bolted the lock, then fell onto the unmade bed. His chest heaved as he regained his composure. Both hands were shaking.

His heart slowly stilled as he listened for sounds in the hallway. Nothing. He was safe . . . this time.

Patrick sighed and emptied his pockets. The first time he'd stolen, it had bothered him. The second time, too. Then, somehow in his mind, he had made it okay. The people had more than him. They could spare some cash. At least that's what he told himself.

Today everything seemed different. The familiar thrill that he got after stealing was gone. He felt trapped in his life, and he was tired of running.

The day before, he had been sitting in the square. He had picked up a sandwich from the soup kitchen and had just found a vacant park bench when a friend of his father appeared beside him. He was a man Patrick knew from childhood—one of his teachers in the village school.

"Paddy?"

Patrick had not been called that name in a while.

"Yes?" He looked up into the weathered face of his old teacher and felt a clench in his heart. "Mr. O'Donnell," he said, suddenly aware of his unshaven face and dirty clothes.

"Paddy, I have a letter for you," Mr. O'Donnell said. He fumbled in his briefcase. "Your father gave it to me in case I saw you here. I've been teaching at the university this term."

Patrick sat still, the uneaten sandwich in his hand. He dropped the sandwich in his lap, wiped a hand on his pant leg, and took the letter. His father's spiderlike handwriting on the front was unmistakable.

"I've carried the letter around for months now, hoping I would see you. We heard—"

Patrick stuffed the letter into his pocket and looked down.

"Thank you," he said abruptly. He didn't want to know what Mr. O'Donnell had heard. When he looked up again, his teacher was gone.

Sitting on the park bench, he read the letter. The letter had news—news that confused him. How could it be possible? How could this have happened? He read it again. Four words stood out to him:

You are needed here.

He had not thought of home in months and suddenly, this. Patrick could not move. He felt weighted down with shame. Even if he was needed, he could never go home now. He had strayed too far. If his father knew the things he had done, he would never have sent the letter. How had it happened?

When he had become a teenager, his father had seemed old and out of touch, disapproving of how Patrick spent his evenings with the young people in the pub, drinking ale and staying out too late. Then came the red-headed girl whom he had liked so much. She was new in town, visiting for the summer, and he'd thought she was the most beautiful creature in the world, with her pale complexion and deep-red lipstick. His father tried to warn him about the dangers of late nights, drunkenness, and girls, but Patrick had stubbornly continued on, spending every evening he could with the girl. Now he could hardly remember her.

With his father growing more and more disappointed in him, the house became uncomfortable, even suffocating. That fall, Patrick left Ireland, slipping away in the night without a word. He had been happy to leave his father's critical eye.

The first night in London was magic. As was the next and the next and the next. Freedom. The girls, the booze, the singing, the dancing. It was a blur of things that had always been forbidden.

Then his money ran out, and Patrick's so-called friends disappeared. The memories of all the cheap hotels and the early days of begging and then stealing were painful now.

He'd love to go home, especially after hearing the news in the letter, but what could he say to his father? How could he ever hope to make up for all that he'd carelessly thrown away? Despite what had seemed so outdated and restricting, there had been a certain freedom there in the suffocating house that he had not found in London.

Sitting up on the side of the bed, Patrick studied his morning's haul. The wallet was worn and not very promising, but at least it was something. He had spotted the two old men as they'd walked away from the Chunnel and had used his favorite technique: the bump and grab.

He looked to see what the old man had in his wallet. Not much. There were a few bills, which he took and put in his pocket; a picture of an older woman, maybe the guy's wife; and a piece of paper. He opened it. Psalm 23. *Great*, Patrick thought, *worthless paper*.

His eyes fell to the middle of the page—*He leads me in paths of righteousness*.

His heart clenched. The words brought back unwanted memories of his father. He closed his eyes and saw the old man's strong shoulders and gray hair. He saw himself, a young Paddy, redheaded and freckled, following his father along the paths in the fields, just like a sheep. There was nothing like the relationship of a father and a son. His chest tightened as he thought about it.

Patrick could almost hear his father's voice filled with emotion.

"Paddy, God wants you goin' down the right path."

The very words that his father had used to teach him now condemned him. His father had wanted the best for him. He could see that now, but back then he only saw it as meddling and old-fashioned.

Patrick put the psalm back in the wallet and tossed

the wallet under the bed out of sight. Funny that it was the shepherd's song. If there was one thing Patrick knew about, it was sheep. He had spent the first eighteen years of his life with sheep. He even slept with them. The lambs that were rejected by their ewes or were too small for the outdoors stayed in his family's small house. Patrick remembered the musty smell of the lambs that slept in his room and the softness of the little ones that curled up next to him.

Every day he took the sheep to the lower pasture. They went down the same trodden path every morning, then again every evening, yet somehow the sheep managed to stray off, then stand puzzled like they were wondering what had happened. Old Bessie was the worst. She had walked the same path all her life, but the day he'd left, she had turned off the path and ended up across the field, looking back at him with a bewildered expression.

He leads me in paths of righteousness.

Patrick was so far from the right path that he didn't know how to get back. He thought about the psalm coming to him in a stolen wallet. Was it a message from God?

"Okay, God," he said, not really expecting a response. "Show me the right path."

"Go back." The thought popped into his mind, like a torch suddenly lighting a dark room.

Everything in him fought against it.

"Go back." The words rang in his head—they would not go away.

You can't go back, he told himself. *You've gone too far.*

But he wanted to go back. He had to go back. The news in the letter changed everything.

He thought about what it was like to be a father separated from your son, and suddenly he could feel the longing of a father—that desire to have your child in your arms. He remembered how he had held the lambs as a boy and how he had loved them. A father could love like that.

"Go home," the voice in his head spoke again. This time, instead of persistent doubts and accusations, a warm spot glowed. Before he could rethink it, Patrick loaded his few belongings in his backpack and left the hotel. He would need to do a few more jobs, just to get enough money to make it home, and then he'd be on his way back to Ireland.

On the street, things seemed dull and confusing. Nothing felt right.

He spotted an elderly couple and knew they would be perfect targets. He moved toward them. They looked a little like his grandparents.

"No." The thought came to him. A single word that seemed to guide him.

"No." He moved past the couple.

"Good day," the man said, tipping his hat.

"Good day," Patrick answered. That feeling came again. That warm spot of light.

A young hitchhiker walked up beside him at the street corner. Her backpack brushed his hand. It was unzipped! Easy pickin's. *"No."* The thought came, and he hesitated.

"Hey," he said to the girl. "You might want to zip that." She looked back at her open pack.

"Can you get it for me?" she asked.

Patrick zipped the pack up. He almost laughed out loud at himself, zipping instead of unzipping a backpack. It felt good.

One after another, he ruled out every good target he saw. Finally, by dinnertime, he was hungry. He pulled out the bills from his pocket and looked at the stolen money. "*It's not yours,*" the voice inside him said. The voice was right. How could he live like this? It was not his money, but he could not give it back, either.

A homeless man leaned on the wall by the café. Patrick gave him the money. It was a relief to have it gone.

It was the right path. He felt sure of it.

"*Go,*" the voice inside him said. But how would he get home without money? And what would be waiting for him at home? Would he be forgiven? In a storybook world the answer was yes, but this was real life—no guarantees.

Patrick stood for a moment and thought about the news in the letter. Then he steeled himself and started walking. He crossed the river, wove through Hyde Park, through neighborhoods and other small parks until he reached the edge of town. There he slept in a green hay field curled up under the clear night sky. When dawn was breaking, he woke and watched the sunrise. Then he continued walking.

Along the way he was overwhelmed with the unexpected generosity that seemed to follow him. A man with a bread truck gave him a ride. Another shared a sandwich. An elderly woman paid his way on the ferry. He knew he did not deserve it. He had been taking things by force for so long that he had forgotten about the goodness that could come from people.

Days passed. Patrick prayed as he walked. It wasn't the formal prayers of the church, just conversations with his shepherd, thoughts that came to him but seemed to emanate from somewhere outside of himself.

Patrick thought of all the things he had done since those days when he was a child with his father, things that brought him shame, and he listed them one by one, confessing as he prayed. Then peace came.

When another stranger picked him up outside Dublin, Patrick was grateful. As they rode across the countryside toward home, he stared out the window and watched the stone walls go by. The hills leading into Cork were green, even greener than he had remembered.

Patrick rubbed his hand over his unshaven face, then smoothed his dirty shirt, wishing he didn't look quite so disheveled and worn. He had no choice. He had to go just as he was.

His anxiety grew as he covered the remaining miles. Over and over he rehearsed in his mind what he would say to his father. He thought again about the news in the letter and how it would change his life forever.

His ride let him off on the north side of town, only a few miles from his father's farm. The walk would give him time to build his courage.

Patrick continued along the narrow road lined with a low stone wall. The fields around him were dotted with sheep, and Patrick thought again about the psalm. *He leads me in paths of righteousness.*

The desire to return home grew stronger. He even longed for the endless chores that he had once dreaded. And he longed to be in the fields once again with the sheep—those dumb, stupid, idiotic sheep. But the most overwhelming desire was the uniting of father and son. Yes, that's what he wanted.

Patrick picked up his pace and began running down the lane. It was the longest mile of the whole trip, but his legs felt strong and his heart felt free. He was at last running *toward* something, not away. The small stone cottage came into view, and he could see the smoke from the chimney and the light in the windows.

As he reached the house, he paused, seized with sudden doubt.

"Knock," the voice said.

He knocked softly and pushed the door open. Sitting by the fireplace, his father looked up, his face older than Patrick remembered. His father stared at him, mouth open.

Patrick tried to begin the words he had rehearsed so many times. Nothing came.

His father stood weakly, tears in his eyes, and held out his arms.

"Paddy, you're finally home."

They embraced—father and son reunited.

"I have so much to tell you," Patrick said. "I'm so sorry for—"

"Later," his father said.

Patrick pulled away and followed his father's eyes to the corner of the room where a small cradle stood by the window. Slowly Patrick crossed the room. He gazed down at the small life in front of him. His son. His own flesh and blood. So beautiful, so perfect. Patrick felt completely amazed.

The words of the letter came back.

You are needed here. You have a son now, and he needs a father.

Patrick reached down and picked up his son, drawing the baby to his chest.

"God wants you goin' down the right path," Patrick whispered into his son's soft ear. "I'll be with you to show you how." He felt the warmth of the baby's breath against his unshaven cheek.

He held the boy back, gazed into his face, and was warmed by the look of guileless acceptance and trust in the baby's eyes. He knew he would never leave again.

There was nothing like the relationship of a father and a son. Patrick wanted to be the kind of father to his son that his father was to him, always loving him and ready to accept him home despite all that he had done. Whatever he needed to do, he would do. Whatever he needed to learn, he would learn. The shepherd had promised to lead him, and at last he was willing to follow.

"Well done." The thought came, affirming and comforting. The running had stopped. Patrick was home.

CHAPTER

Seven

---

*Even though I walk through
the valley of the shadow of death*

WHAT'S THE BEST WAY to kill myself?

The question loomed large in front of Jake. The walls of his seedy London hotel room seemed like a tomb, like he was already dead. He took off his glasses, ran his hands through his salt-and-pepper hair, rubbed his unshaven chin. How should he do it?

Gun? Too complicated. He had never owned a weapon. He couldn't imagine buying one now.

Jump off a bridge? Too dramatic. And what if he lived?

Knife? Too messy. All that blood.

Two weeks ago he seemed to have it all. Perfect wife. Perfect job. Perfect life . . . on the outside. What would his wife, June, think if she could see him now? It didn't matter. All he had left of her was the note she had left behind. She would likely file for divorce soon. And his job—two weeks ago he was a man of reputation, a man realizing his ambitions. Now it was all gone. He was about as low as a man could go. Jake wanted relief from the disappointment, the feelings of rejection and emptiness.

Pills? Yes, pills would be perfect. Going quietly. And he had plenty of those with him. His doctor had prescribed the pills to help him sleep. He looked at the small bottle in his hand. These pills would not fix the deep pit that his life had become unless he took all of them.

The hotel room was dreary. Jake lay back on the lumpy bed and tried not to think. He didn't want to die in this depressing room. He hated the thought of June hearing that he went like this. He wanted to be outside, somewhere beautiful, at the end. But where? He saw a pile of tourist brochures on the desk. He reached over and picked up the first one.

El Camino de Santiago. "The Way of St. James." One hundred kilometers of trails through France and Spain, hiked by millions of people for hundreds of years.

Medieval pilgrims had made the journey for spiritual reasons, but it would not be a spiritual journey for Jake. He didn't need that. For him it was an escape, and, more important, it was the perfect place for his last good-bye on earth. Tomorrow he would travel to France to begin.

Jake felt a sense of purpose. He began to pack his few belongings. As he reached down to gather the dirty clothes on the floor, something under the bed caught his eye. It was a wallet. He pulled it out. It was empty except for a couple of photos and a folded piece of paper. He opened the paper and saw the words of the twenty-third psalm. His eyes fell on the line, *Even though I walk through the valley of the shadow of death.* He clenched his fist and shook it at the ceiling.

"Don't even try," he said to God. "Don't even try!" Someone in the room next door pounded on the wall, and Jake realized that he had been yelling.

He crumpled the paper into a ball and threw it out the window. He looked out in time to see it fall into the unsuspecting hands of a young man with a Mohawk haircut.

Good, Jake thought. *Maybe it'll mean something to that guy.*

He slammed the window shut. He was finished with God and Bible verses and trying to do right. Where had it gotten him but here?

Tomorrow he would walk.

There was a relief in that—the idea of just walking. He didn't have to figure out how to do life. He didn't have to talk to anyone. He didn't have to help anyone. He didn't have to organize anyone. He didn't even have to look at anyone. One foot in front of the other. That was all he had to do, and soon he could stop walking for good.

In the morning Jake traveled to France. He purchased a backpack, bedroll, walking stick, and water bottle at a small store that catered to pilgrims, those making the walk to Santiago de Compostela. He slipped the bottle of pills into the side pocket of the backpack. He was ready. With the help of the store owner he found the start of the Camino trail.

Somehow he expected it to be better marked, but there it was—only a small wooden sign with a seashell, the Camino symbol, pointing in the direction of the path. He took his walking stick and left the road.

A light rain fell, and Jake put on his hat as he started up the path. The dreariness of the rain seemed proper and right. His feet crunched on the gravel. His pack felt good against his back, not too heavy.

Up ahead he saw other pilgrims. When he saw them, he slowed his place. He did not want to know anything about them. Their stooped shoulders made them look so vulnerable. If he met them, they would begin to pour out their pain on him, and it would be too much. Jake had heard enough sad stories in his life. When he thought of it, his shoulders hurt. He stopped to rub each shoulder. He had his own pain to deal with.

He remembered his last day of work.

"We need to talk," Arthur had said.

Jake had been intrigued. *What could Arthur want?* He respected Arthur and knew Arthur respected him. Perhaps Arthur was giving him more responsibility. Jake had given the secretary the thumbs-up sign as he'd gone into Arthur's office. Later he remembered the sad look on her face. She had not returned the sign.

"We're going to have to let you go," Arthur had said.

"Where?" Jake had asked, and then the awful truth had dawned on him. He was not being sent on a trip; he was being fired. All the extra hours. All the weekends. All the missed vacations and holidays. All for nothing.

"It's not you," Arthur continued. "It's budget cuts . . . the economy."

Jake had not seen it coming. He had even told June they couldn't go on vacation this year, that he had to work. He remembered with a sinking feeling that he had actually said to her, "Don't you understand, my job is my life?"

That night Jake had walked the city streets until late, then he had gone home like nothing had happened. He couldn't tell June. There was no one in his world he could tell. All his support had been at work. All his friends were there. All his value had come from there.

The rain stopped, and the sun emerged. He climbed steadily upward on the steep path. No one traveled with him today, yet he had the constant feeling of being followed. Was he becoming paranoid? He concentrated on the path, watching his feet.

The sun was hot, and he found himself stopping often to drink water and look at the map. He seemed to be making almost no progress, and it was becoming an effort to keep going. Several times he looked back, but there was nothing there for him.

The first day ended as Jake walked to one of the stations. There were beds, and for dinner, a stew. When he fell into the bed, he thought about the day and decided he was sorry he had started the whole thing. It was harder than he'd thought, and his feet ached.

Jake lay awake, wide-eyed. He couldn't sleep with crowds of people sharing the room, coughing and snoring. He longed for morning to come, and when it finally arrived, he got up early, only to find a long line for the bathroom. After he packed his things, he took the bread and cheese that was offered to him and left. A small group of pilgrims had gathered outside to sing a hymn. He walked around them without stopping.

His muscles ached from the miles he had walked the day before, and his shoulders hurt from carrying his load. Regardless of the problems, he was determined to keep going. As usual, it was his determination that would move him forward.

"I will walk today. I will put one foot in front of the other. I will not think. I will not feel. I will just walk."

The sound of the singing pilgrims took him back to the beginning of his journey of faith. It had been everything to him. He was a young student at summer camp when he had discovered Jesus and given his life to Him. The moment was clear, and in the middle of many teenage memories that were incomplete or blurred with time, this one was etched in his mind as if it had happened just yesterday.

Out under the trees and stars one splendid night, the youth pastor had talked about God and his love for everyone. Jake was overwhelmed with the feeling of love, and in that moment his life changed. He had been so sure of what God wanted from him. "I surrender all," he had sung, and he'd meant every word.

He climbed steadily upward on the steep path. No one else was walking nearby, yet once again he had the feeling of being followed. Was he losing his mind? He needed to concentrate on the path and stop thinking.

A young couple passed him, laughing and holding hands. Meeting June had been one of the great moments of his life. June was there the year he found God, and they fell in love that summer. It all seemed perfectly planned. She was beautiful, with her curly brown hair and the flowered dresses she always wore. He had fallen fast and hard. They'd seemed to have it all. How could he have lost her?

The walk continued through a strand of trees. Jake stopped a moment in the shade. When the job had come open in the town of Brownstone, it seemed that God was leading him and providing for his family. He put his life into his job. Isn't that what God wanted? Hard work.

Every choice seemed to be divinely directed—marriage, job, success. Choice by choice he had built his life.

The day stretched on. He walked alone.

Jake continued going higher. Again he had the feeling of being followed. He stopped several times to look behind him, but no one was there.

In the quiet he realized there were things that he had missed the days before. The smell of pine needles, the call of birds. He heard one bird that he recognized from growing up in Lancaster, a jay of some kind. Another call from a small, brown bird that peeked at him from a berry bush.

A sparrow, he thought. He watched the sparrow pick a berry and fly higher to eat. He wished that he could be a sparrow. Something about the simplicity of the bird's life appealed to him. Birds lived with other birds, but they lived in harmony, not dependence, just living together. Why couldn't the world be like that?

"Even a sparrow has found a home." He remembered the scripture but put it out of his mind. No more Bible verses. He was done with God and all that Bible stuff.

He passed two older women, who walked slowly, leaning on their walking sticks. He nodded. They nodded back, and it felt okay to have them nearby, but silent.

That night in the small pension, Jake was alone. He wrapped himself in his bedroll and looked out the small window at the slice of moon in the sky. Finally he slept. A few hours later he woke. Again he felt that prickling sensation that he was not alone. Perhaps someone else had come in during the night.

"Anyone there?" he called out.

No answer.

He could not get back to sleep.

Morning came, and he started out again.

He walked on the path, his mind empty. He saw a woman with a large cross hanging around her neck stopped on the path ahead.

The woman did not look at Jake. She simply pointed ahead. "A valley of cairns."

Jake stared out at the valley filled with stones, thousands and thousands of them. Some standing alone; many stacked into small towers.

"The stones represent the pain," she said. "People leave them behind. It is the end of pain and the beginning of life."

And for me, Jake thought, *it will be the end of both.*

"Did you bring a stone?" the woman asked. "Everyone leaves something behind here."

Jake shook his head. He watched as the woman walked forward and placed a small white stone on top of one of the piles, then she continued on the path.

He sat under a large tree and rested his back on the rough bark. There were stones everywhere stacked on top of one another. Sometimes two, sometimes many, balanced and stable. *Man's need to make his mark.* Jake thought. *Or perhaps it's man's need to reach up to God.* He thought of his own strivings, of his attempts to be noticed and to gain recognition—always the need for significance. What had it come to? Nothing.

He watched a young woman balancing a small stone

atop a large flat stone. He saw an older couple walk by and add two turquoise stones to a pile. They paused in silence, or maybe in prayer, then continued on.

He imagined that the stones were from all over the world. Thousands of pains left behind. Burdens that seemed so heavy, overwhelming.

Darkness came, and Jake closed his eyes. Tonight he would spend the night outside under the stars. At dawn he would do it—end his life.

Later that night Jake again felt a presence. He ignored it and stared at the sky. The stars were incredible. Bright and vast. *The heavens declare the glory of God*, Jake thought, before he could stop himself.

"Leave me alone!" he cried to the night and the stars. "Leave me alone."

He rose and stared at the sky. Silence and the overwhelming beauty of the stars pierced his heart.

Even though I walk through the valley of the shadow of death.

Jake remembered the words of the psalm that he had read in the hotel room.

"Here I am in the valley!" he shouted. "Are you with me? Are you with me now? Do you even care?!"

Moonlight lit the path, and, exhausted, Jake dropped to his knees and wept.

"Why, God? Why weren't you with me? How could you do this to me?"

There was no answer except the stars and the moonlight and the piles of rocks reaching up and the words in his mind.

Even though I walk through the valley of the shadow of death.

"You let me down! You deserted me!"

He yelled the words into the emptiness around him.

The silence made the anger worse. "Won't you even answer me?" he yelled at the sky.

Silence. Only the gleaming stars. Suddenly he felt so small. A tiny human man dwarfed by the universe.

The millions of stars, galaxies, and the universe spoke of the hugeness of God. Jake's smallness mirrored the smallness of his own understanding.

And the memory came back to him of the night he first believed. God had met him in the words of the youth pastor, and God's love had been so real. The stars had shone above him just like this night.

God had not asked him to take the job. God had not required the weekends of work, the canceled vacations, nor neglecting his wife.

The stars still beamed down all these years later, offering him love. In his deepest valley, God was still here.

Even though I walk through the valley of the shadow of death.

How pitiful. He was running away from his life and God. God had never left him. He had left God. He wept.

His anger abated, and he sat for a long time looking at the heavens and the piles of rocks.

"I surrender all," he said finally, echoing the words he had sung as a young student.

Slowly, the mysterious presence that had followed him for days, maybe even for years, settled on him and engulfed him, wrapping around his tired shoulders like a shawl. Jake sank into the peace of God. He slept.

Morning broke. The sun peeked over the horizon and

glinted off the stones in the valley. He had known so much about God, but he had never known God . . . till now. Jacob walked through the valley and chose a large, solid stone. He carried it back and placed it on the spot where he had wept.

"God," he said, "from now on you will be my foundation, nothing else!"

He found a smooth stone and placed it on the rock. "I'm resting on you, God. Not my job or Arthur, but you."

He found one more rock, a small, perfect, beautiful round stone, and placed it on top of the other two.

"Thank you for June. You have given me my wife. If there's any way possible, I will work it out. If not, I will let her go."

He looked out at the field of need and pain, thousands of small towers, representing thousands of needs. His heart was tendered by the stacks of stone, the need of people for hope. The need for someone to share hope.

"I will go where you send me."

He remembered the psalm in the hotel room and his anger. A piece of paper in a seedy hotel room had brought him God's word and reminded him he was not alone.

He pulled out the bottle of pills. This was the place he had decided to end his life. Jake opened the bottle and poured the pills into his hand. He stared at the little, round white circles.

"God, I surrender," he said. "I give you my past."

He remembered his decision to become a minister, his seminary training, his ordination, and his call to

Brownstone Church. He thought of the hurt he had experienced in his rejection from the church—his firing by Reverend Arthur.

"I give you my present."

Jake thought about this trip and his choice to live. In one sweeping throw he hurled the pills out into the field.

"I give you my future."

He thought of the many people who needed to hear about God's love. He was being given a fresh start. He felt energized at the thought of sharing the truth of Christ's love to those hurting and in need.

Reverend Jake Ford lifted his arms toward heaven and declared, "Praise God from whom all blessings flow."

He picked up his walking stick and turned toward a small village in the distance. He breathed the fresh morning air and realized that something was different. He wanted to live. He would call June as soon as possible and tell her everything.

God was with him, and the rest of his life was ahead.

CHAPTER
Eight

I will fear no evil, for you are with me

MARRA GLANCED NERVOUSLY out the window of Johnny's Tattoo Parlor. She felt vulnerable sitting in the metal chair, wrapped in a sheet worn soft from many launderings. The sheet was draped to one side, like a Roman toga, exposing her left arm and upper back. She pushed her chair further out of the line of sight of passersby on the street, although there was only one passerby that mattered. Lobo.

This was a small shop in Barcelona near the docks, not a place he would likely look for her, but she couldn't be sure. Lobo was smart, and he had a sixth sense about people.

She shivered a little in the coolness of the room and reached for her scarf. She wrapped it around her small shoulders and took a deep breath. The smell of latex and astringent were familiar and comforting, but not enough to quell the fear rising within her—the fear of evil. Lobo's own special brand of evil.

Rock music blared from the speakers, and she could hear Johnny, the tattoo artist and shop owner, arguing on the phone in the back. *Girl trouble*, she thought. How well she understood. She touched the bruise on her cheek and remembered the pain of Lobo's fist.

"You want something to drink?" Johnny called.

"No."

In Marra's mind loomed a question, growing by the minute. It was a question she'd asked herself over and over during the past year—soon she would have the answer. She glanced at the clock on the wall. 9:15. She was to board the ship at 11:15. In two hours she would know the answer to her question: Could she leave Lobo? Could she really go through with it? Or would she hurry back, hopefully before he knew she was gone?

Marra pushed away thoughts of Lobo. She wanted to think about her new tattoo. Choosing the right tattoo had always been a challenge, and it was one of the few things she did right in her life.

She ran her hand over her right forearm, touching the design of a two-headed dragon exhaling flames up the side of her arm, smoke trailing behind—her first tattoo, representing her parents who had put her out on the street on her eighteenth birthday. She couldn't tell anyone what she had experienced living with them—the pain and shame were too much to share, the scars too deep within. So, she had shown it on her body.

Good ole Mom and Dad, she thought, looking at the two-headed monster.

"Decided what you want?" Johnny called.

"Not yet."

She looked at the walls surrounding her, covered with endless possibilities—cartoon characters and political figures, kittens and grizzly bears, zodiac signs, pin-up girls, hearts with banners that said *Mom*. Magazines and books with more designs covered the tables.

The shop bell rang, and Marra jumped off her chair,

whirling around to face the door and possibly Lobo. Instead, it was three giggling girls.

"I think it's soooo cool," one said.

"I vote for SpongeBob."

They giggled as they made their way to the wall. Then they caught sight of Marra with her jet-black hair pinned on top of her head and her powder-white skin covered in tattoos. Their eyes widened. One girl whispered to the others, and they laughed nervously, taking a wide arc around Marra.

Marra sat back on the chair, this time vowing to be more alert and to keep a closer watch on the door. She'd need to be extra cautious. She took note of the back door and how she could get away if Lobo showed up.

The three girls studied the tattoo possibilities, pointing and laughing.

Marra stretched out her leg, and one graceful ankle came into view. A dark-green serpent twined around the ankle and up her calf. Her second tattoo. How could she tell anyone about her boss at the sandwich shop, the way he had touched her when the customers were gone? He was a serpent.

Her body was covered with tattoos, with things unsaid. Something in her longed to speak, but the words could not form. *Abuse victims lose their voice*, she'd read in an article about trauma. It was true.

Now she had another story to tell. Her life was changing again. She was leaving Lobo . . . maybe. Another girl had left him once. Marra had heard stories of how he had found her, of the ugly results of his rage. Marra had left him twice herself, but always ran back, even before he knew she was gone.

What tattoo could tell the story of her life with Lobo? Nothing here could capture the darkness. She had been drawn in by his strength and power. The dark blue-black of his skin and the sculpted muscles that seemed to offer protection . . . at first. He seemed to have it all, and every girl wanted Lobo.

She'd seen him first when he'd come into the Silver Bullet. He had seemed so beautiful. His dark skin had glowed in the incandescent light of the bar. She'd wondered at the glimmer of something dark hidden behind the black eyes. Marra had poured him a drink and watched his eyes assess her body. Why was she drawn to him?

"You want anything else?" she had asked.

"Yeah," he'd answered in his deep, sultry voice, taking all of her in. When she'd left for the night, he had been waiting, and she had been with him ever since.

Johnny emerged from the back. "I'll be with you in a minute," he said to Marra. He turned to the girls. "What can I do for you?"

"I want Tweety Bird."

"Ray does a great Tweety Bird," Johnny said, and he called to the back, "Ray."

Ray appeared and led the girls to the empty chair across the room.

Johnny sat down and rolled his chair forward to Marra. His white T-shirt and jeans were clean and his hair neatly shaved into a Mohawk. A single tattoo, a small black cross, peeked out from his upper arm. Everyone said he was the best.

"Hey," he said.

She liked his easy way and friendly eyes.

"Hi."

She removed the scarf and let it fall to the back of the chair. She lowered her gaze.

Johnny touched the jagged scar across her shoulder. "How'd you get that?"

She didn't flinch. "My old man did it."

Johnny let out a low whistle.

"Some old man. You don't still live with him?" He looked at her seriously.

Marra shook her head. "I moved out when I was eighteen. That scar was from years ago. I was only five."

"Evil."

She nodded, unable to deny it about her own father.

"Marra! Get out of the way." Whack! Her father had slapped her across the back. "I said, get out of the way!" He pulled back and, with all his might, swung. She had dodged his fist but lost her balance and fell onto the glass coffee table, which broke and sliced into her shoulder.

"Here." Johnny showed her a T-shaped scar on his temple. "Here's mine. Courtesy of my brother."

The corners of her mouth turned up. It was as much of a smile as she ever gave.

"Yeah, evil."

"This one's not old." Johnny touched her cheek.

Marra flushed deep red but could not talk. Johnny didn't pursue it. He glanced at the form she had filled out.

"Marra. Let's see what you got."

Marra stretched out her arms. The paleness of her skin seemed so white in comparison to the jet-black ink that adorned her left wrist and forearm. The lace pattern formed a thick bracelet of fine interwoven lines, like gossamer threads, but distinct. Up the arm the pattern continued in graceful, black lacy swirls.

Johnny nodded. "Nice. Delicate looking."

"That's what I was going for."

The lace covering her left arm told of a coat of armor—the protection that she could not ask for.

Eighteen, alone and on the streets, she had asked her guidance counselor for help. Instead of help, she got more abuse.

She couldn't tell Johnny that she'd lived with fear and evil most of her life and that she had been trying to quash the fear by slowly, piece by piece, tattooing her entire body.

"What do you want this time?"

"I'm leaving Barcelona tonight . . . maybe." She paused, deciding how much to tell him. "Bartending on a cruise ship. I'm starting over, kind of. I think. I want a tattoo . . . to show where I am in my life."

The cruise would be a way to start again, leaving behind the hell of her own choices. Her relationship with Lobo had circled in a world of heroin use and crime. This morning, when she had complained about the drugs, Lobo had become angry. "Don't tell me what to do. You're nothing." His fist surprised her, knocking her to the floor. "You hear me? You're nothing!"

His words confirmed what she had always known.

When she had heard that the cruise ship was looking for bartenders, she hadn't hesitated. Last night she had applied using her cell phone and got the call back within an hour. She looked again at the clock. Now it was 9:30. She had to avoid Lobo for another hour and forty-five minutes.

A shiver of fear went down her spine. He would kill her if he knew. At least he might not find her here at Johnny's . . . maybe. Lobo was smart. He always seemed to be a step ahead of everyone else. She shivered again.

Johnny didn't seem to notice. "Show me what you want and where you want it."

"Here." She showed him one of the few clear places on her leg. "Can you do something here?"

Johnny rolled closer on his stool. His touch on her skin was gentle. She thought of all the hurt that other touches had caused her, including the scar.

"Sure. What design?" Johnny pointed to some possibilities on the wall. "I could do a ship and anchor, like that—to represent the cruise."

"No."

"Martini glass?"

"No."

"Or an eagle with its wings spread out? New beginnings."

"No."

Marra wasn't sure what she wanted this time. In the past it had been easy to choose tattoos to tell the stories of her life—the darkness, the pain. The tattoo of two black teardrops coming down from her eye were for Emmie, the friend she lost to heroin. The fireballs on her back were when she had been burned by an angry lover. And so on, until the tattoos began to overlap and there was little skin left unmarked.

Some tattoos she got just because she liked the pain. When she was getting a tattoo, the pain took over. It descended like a blanket, smothering out the memories and thoughts that haunted her and filling the emptiness inside.

Now Marra was ready for something different. This time the design had to be right.

"I'll go with the chain." She pointed to links of chain on the wall. It wasn't exactly what she wanted, but it seemed a good choice. She had been in bondage so long that it was almost physical. "Can you make it wrap all the way around?"

"Yeah. Good idea."

He began to get out his things. He showed her the sterile packs of needles and got out his tattoo gun.

She looked at the chain and thought how tired she was of fear and pain and evil. Would she have to run forever? How could she break the chains?

Her eyes wandered across the room to the bulletin board covered with pictures of happy clients displaying ships and yin-yangs. One sheet of paper stood out from the rest.

"Psalm 23," she read. "What's that doing up there?"

The paper had been crumpled but was smoothed out now. It was covered with the carefully printed words of the psalm.

Johnny shrugged, "I was walking down a sidewalk in London when it just fell out of the sky." Her brow wrinkled. "Okay, someone threw it out of a hotel window. I thought it might make a good tattoo. The verses and all. People like stuff like that."

He got up. "I've got to get the chain pattern from the file." He headed to the back room.

While he was gone, Marra took the psalm from the board and scanned the words.

"'I will fear no evil,'" she read out loud, then laughed. "I've feared evil all my life." She read the next line. "'For you are with me.'"

It was a hard thought. Was God with her during those dark times? She had never thought about God. Was it possible that there was a God? She wished it could be true. Was God good? If only it could be so.

Up until now she did not believe in God. It was easier that way—one less person in the world to let her down.

Marra stared at the psalm. *I will fear no evil, for you are with me.*

The door jingled. Fear and panic grabbed her chest like a vise as she imagined Lobo's dark eyes glaring and him yelling, "You're nothing!" But it was only the girls leaving. Marra didn't want this kind of fear anymore. There had to be something different.

The words of the psalm were copied by hand; it looked like a woman's writing. She wondered about the woman who had written the words and the faith that she must have had to print them so carefully.

There was a tenderness in the thought. *Help me believe, too*, Marra thought, and she realized that she was praying. She smiled at the thought that she was praying to a God that she did not believe existed.

"Okay," she acknowledged to the empty room. The corners of her mouth turned up again. "I believe that you exist."

The prayer was a start, and in an odd way it made her feel calmer. She let out a deep breath and sat in a quiet moment, looking at the paper.

Johnny came back, sat, and rolled the chair forward. He held the chain pattern up to her skin.

"I think I can probably get eight, maybe ten links on there."

"Wait."

Johnny rolled back. "You change your mind?"

She nodded.

"It's okay. You can come back another time."

"No, I think I want to try something different. I've had enough of chains and stuff."

"We got plenty more. We could get out the catalogs."

"No, I want this." She held out the paper.

"The psalm?"

"Yes."

"All of it?"

"No. That line, there. 'I will fear no evil, for you are with me.'"

Johnny nodded, studying the words.

"Yeah. Yeah, I can see it. A scroll with the words inside on two lines. With letters that aren't too ornate. You want to be able to read it." He smiled broadly. "I like it!"

She gave him a small smile, a little bigger this time.

"I like it, too." And suddenly she did. She longed for the God who would take away her fear by His very presence.

"Can you put it here?" She showed him a new location.

"Interesting choice," he said. He ran his fingers over the area and studied it closely. Then he nodded.

"Not easy, but I can do it."

He drew the pattern, and she nodded her approval.

He gently shaved the area to prepare the skin. The antiseptic gel was cold and soothing. He pressed the pattern on the damp area and pulled it off to leave the image of the words behind.

Johnny began working, taking his time with each letter. Marra watched in the mirror. She could see the needles tapping, doing their job. The work was slow, and Johnny took his time. The tattoo took shape.

As the words became a permanent part of her, she felt more and more empowered by them. *I will fear no evil, for you are with me.* With God beside her, she would no longer fear evil. After all, God was the one who created everything. He was powerful—more powerful than her father, more powerful than her old boyfriends, or her previous employers, or anyone, even Lobo. With God she had nothing to fear.

Johnny dabbed off the last of the ink, then held up a mirror for her to see. In the mirror she saw herself differently. Confident. Fearless. Worthy.

She gazed at the final result. Covering her long, jagged scar was a scroll inset with the words:

I will fear no evil,
for you are with me.

The scar had been transformed. No longer visible.

Johnny smiled, obviously pleased with the results. "What do you think?" he asked.

"I will fear no evil," she answered.

She felt a curl of courage growing inside her, along with another emotion she had not felt before, something warm, like the sunlight, and bright and open and spacious—love. It could be love. God loved her.

Marra looked at the clock. 10:45.

"Do you have a minute?" she asked.

"All day."

She looked at the tattoos covering her body. One by one she told Johnny her stories, starting with the first, and going forward, until they both sat weeping. It felt good to tell her stories. Suddenly the power of telling engulfed her. She was energized by the thought that there were more people out there—other women—who needed to hear her story. They needed courage and the strength of God with them.

Her final tattoo would be with her always, to remind her of the fact that she didn't have to fear anymore because God was with her.

Johnny was still wiping his eyes when he handed her the psalm.

"You turned me into a big marshmallow."

"I think you were already a big marshmallow." She kissed his forehead.

"You keep this." He handed her the psalm. "And here's a coupon for next time."

Marra smiled at him. This time her mouth stretched into a full, wide grin.

"Thanks. I don't think there will be a next time. But I'll take the psalm. I'm sure there's someone else out there who needs it."

Marra left the scarf on the chair and walked to the shop door. She looked out into the sunlight. Lobo was out there somewhere, but she was no longer afraid. The curl of courage inside her was growing. She pushed open the door and stepped outside.

With her head held high Marra walked past the stores toward the ship. For now, the fear inside was gone. There was no pain, just warmth. She would begin again with God; she felt it. She could leave the fear behind and move ahead.

Then she saw him—Lobo, darting in and out of the shops with that angry look on his face, probably looking for her. She stopped for a moment, staring at him. His anger was apparent, his face contorted in rage, his fists balled up as if ready to strike. She no longer saw him as beautiful; she saw him as he was—an angry, evil man filled with bitterness. Her problem—Lobo—was between her and the pier. She glanced down at her new tattoo.

"I will fear no evil," she said out loud. God was bigger than Lobo. God would protect her. Her new strength empowered her, and she walked forward.

Protect me, God, she prayed as she walked straight ahead. She did not cower, or weave in and out of the crowds, or duck into shops, hiding.

She could not explain this new feeling of courage. God was with her; she was sure of it. He would protect her.

As she got closer to Lobo, she prayed, *God, I will fear no evil, for You are with me. I will fear no evil, for You are with me.*

Lobo stopped in the middle of the street, looking right and left.

Marra continued praying as she approached him. She saw his flashing eyes; the muscles of his neck bulged out as he breathed. She was within a few feet of him, but he did not see her. He seemed to be looking everywhere except at her.

The loud bellow of the ship's horn sounded, calling people to board. She took a deep breath and marched around Lobo. As she passed, she smelled his anger, his evil. He turned his head, but his eyes were empty and stared right through her. At the edge of the pier she stopped. She turned to see Lobo storm away into the crowd.

Marra turned her face upward and smiled. She had never seen the sky so blue, the sun so yellow, or the clouds so big and white.

"Thank you," she whispered. Then she hurried down the pier to her new life: transformed, loved, and unafraid.

CHAPTER

Nine

Your rod and your staff,
they comfort me

$\mathcal{T}$HE GUN SOUNDED. Thousands of feet hit the pavement. The Rome Invitational Marathon had begun.

Kioni's feet pounded hard as she reached her stride. The front-runners moved forward as one—Kioni from Kenya, two girls from the United States, one girl from Italy, and the German girl.

The sideline was a mass of color and movement as spectators cheered and waved the flags of many countries.

"Go, Kioni. Go, my girl. Run for Kenya!" Sister Immaculata cheered.

Kioni didn't usually see the spectators, but Sister Immaculata was hard to miss. Her ample body took up two or three seats on the bench, and her big arms fanned her face with a never-ending sway of paper in an attempt to be cool. She lifted her cane as she cheered. It was the cane she used for support—and not just any cane, but a gnarly stick from the forest of Africa.

Kioni's legs stretched and loosened as she made the first mile. *Only twenty-five more to go.*

Her mind shifted. The streets of Italy disappeared, and suddenly she was running on the red dirt roads of Kenya—the twenty-six-mile loop that she ran for training. The grays and the blacks of the city were gone, and the greens of the beautiful Great Rift Valley appeared. In her mind in Africa it was early morning with a huge orange sun rising on the horizon. Thoughts of Africa brought her comfort.

The paper that she had tucked into the back pocket of her shorts brought her comfort, too. It came from a little boy on the street.

"Autograph," he had said, calling up to the window when her bus to the stadium stopped.

"No paper," Kioni said, holding up her empty hands.

The boy darted from person to person along the sidewalks until he found someone, a tattooed girl, to give him a piece of paper. He handed the paper through the bus window to Kioni, but as she searched for a pen, the traffic light turned green and the bus drove away, leaving the boy on the curb and Kioni holding the paper.

"Meet me at the end," she had called, and his smiling face nodded.

On the back of the paper was Psalm 23.

Just the comfort Kioni needed now, for this race, especially when she thought about the German girl who might try to keep her from winning.

Your rod and your staff, they comfort me. The idea of the rod and its protection was not new for Kioni. The shepherds in Africa used rods for protection, and Sister Immaculata's cane was like a staff, guiding Kioni and the other girls at the orphanage.

Some of the slower runners were falling behind, but Kioni was still in the gaggle, out front with the Americans and the Italian, and, of course, the German, who was lagging behind. Often serious opponents did that—stayed behind just far enough so you didn't worry about them. Then, at the end, they would make their move. Kioni shoved that thought from her mind.

Focus. Stay calm.

She was almost to mile five. Where would she be at mile five in Africa?

Ahh. The high trail. She would be on the high trail running through the tall grasses. It was the place where she first saw Runo tending his father's sheep. He had been standing tall with his shepherd's rod in his hand. Her heart had beaten faster as she'd approached the handsome man.

Then she'd seen the elephants blocking her path up ahead. It was unusual to see them there and not down by the stream where they often went for water. The large male in front was upset, breathing hard and stomping his feet. Kioni had stopped running and stepped closer to see what was the matter.

A cobra had risen up beside her on the path. Its head darted forward. Kioni jumped fast. Then Runo appeared and struck with his rod. Whoosh. Snap. The terror was over before it began.

Kioni had stared with mouth open, eyes big. "You killed the snake," she said.

He smiled, showing a mouth full of straight white teeth. "The elephants saw what you could not." Then he laughed, and she laughed, and that's when she fell in love.

Kioni passed mile five. Thinking about the gold and green of the grasses brought the rhythm of her heart into line with the rhythm of her feet.

"Go, Kioni!" she heard Sister Immaculata yell. Sister was waiting at the five-mile mark. The twenty-six-mile course looped back by the stadium twice, and Sister planned to be at both locations when Kioni passed.

"Go, Kenya!" In a flash Kioni ran by. She caught a glimpse of Sister waving her cane.

When they had arrived at the stadium, Sister Immaculata had parted the crowd with her cane.

"Make way!" she had called out. "Make way for Kenya."

Kioni had giggled. "Like Moses parting the Red Sea . . . only more determined even than Moses."

The race continued. The streets of Rome were not so crowded, and there were fewer runners with her now— just the girls from the United States, the Italian, and the German. The German would probably make her move at the end. *Don't think about the end now, only the next mile. That's how you win, one mile at a time.*

Kioni's mind returned to Africa. Across the African plains she ran like a gazelle. Her bare feet pounded a steady rhythm as she lightly flew along the paths and the dry, dusty roadways of Kenya. The ten-mile marker would appear soon. In Africa, the ten-mile mark of her training run meant passing the small village where Kioni had made the decision to marry Runo.

Runo and Kioni and some of the girls from the orphanage had been in the village getting supplies when they'd seen a crowd gathered in front of the outdoor restaurant. They came closer and saw what captivated everyone's attention—a small TV showing a parade. Floats went by, and a drum team, then more floats and marching bands. The majorettes were twirling their batons, tossing them high, and catching them with perfect precision. Kioni and the girls were mesmerized.

Then suddenly, out of the corner of her eye, Kioni saw Runo get up. He marched to the front beside the TV and lifted his rod. All eyes left the TV and focused on Runo. He began twirling his rod in a perfect imitation of the majorettes.

"Go, Runo!" everyone cheered and clapped. Then suddenly he slowed his twirl. He glanced skyward. Everyone got quiet. Kioni held her breath. What was Runo doing? In a great whoosh, he rotated his rod in a circle, then threw it into the air. End over end it rose higher and higher against the blue Kenyan sky. It arced, then started down. Everyone stared, the TV parade forgotten. End over end it descended, everyone hoping against hope it would be caught. Then, just before it hit the ground, Runo grabbed it and twirled it three more times. He closed in a deep bow.

The small band of friends erupted into great cheers. That's when Kioni decided she wanted to marry Runo.

He had asked several times before, but she had hesitated. There were some significant obstacles to marrying Runo. Life seemed always to be full of obstacles. She wished that she could clear them away as easily as Sister moved away the crowd with her cane.

Slap. Slap. Slap. Kioni passed mile ten in the neighborhoods of Rome, her stride in perfect rhythm. Her feet landed firmly with each step. She kept pace with the front-runners. One of the Americans lagged behind a bit. The other American and the Italian were right with her. She did not turn to see the German girl, but she could hear her, running fast, breathing hard, just behind them.

Kioni moved smoothly and carefully, always aware of the position of the German—Gilda was her name. Last year Gilda had taken out the front-runner by shifting closer and closer, then grabbing the opponent's elbow and pulling her back. She did it slyly, where it was difficult for anyone else to see.

Kioni increased her pace. She wished she could hear Sister's voice now, but Sister would not appear again until mile twenty.

With mile fifteen came a calm. Kioni's rhythm was established, and she thought of mile fifteen in Africa— the open plains. Kioni imagined the Cherangani Hills in the distance. She and Runo walked these hills when they talked of marriage and the obstacles that stood in their way. Mostly there was one obstacle: Runo's parents.

"No son of mine will marry a girl from the orphanage," his father had said. "You will marry from a good family, and you will run my sheep farm."

Runo's father would disown him if they married. Runo loved the sheep. Kioni could not take that away from him. Runo was the perfect shepherd. He had a sixth sense about the sheep. He knew when they were in trouble, which was most of the time. Many nights he slept in the field with his sheep, protecting them from other animals. How could he leave them for her? It seemed that there was no easy answer.

The heat of Rome brought her back. Water station. Kioni reached out her hand as she passed and accepted a paper cup of cool water. She drank, then dropped the cup and kept moving. At eighteen miles she heard a gasp and a thud—the American fell.

Focus. Keep the focus on Africa.

Kioni settled her mind on her running path in Africa, on the banyan tree, her favorite tree, making a graceful silhouette against the backdrop of the plains. She remembered one time walking by the tree with Runo. They had been so carefree, even skipping. Then suddenly Runo stopped. "I forgot my rod."

Kioni stopped beside him. She scanned the grass around her. The grass moved . . . or was it the wind . . . or an animal sneaking up, hoping to make them his supper? Without Runo's rod they were defenseless.

"Let's head back now," he said, and they had hurried away.

What a difference one rod made. One minute they were relaxed and lighthearted, the next, overcome with fear. The rod gave them comfort.

Muscle fatigue. At mile nineteen Kioni felt a twinge in her right calf muscle. The heat was taking its toll. She thought of the paper in her pocket. The psalm. The psalm about the shepherd. *God is the shepherd. God has a rod like Runo.* Could God protect her here in Italy, far from home? Could He protect her from Gilda, the German?

Kioni pushed on. Few runners were near now. The

Italian girl had dropped behind. The other American lagged, too, but held close. Gilda, the German, was moving closer. Kioni's legs pumped up and down like pistons, as she pulled away to solidify her lead.

Sister would be at the twenty-mile mark. Kioni wanted to see Sister. Sister had supported her and loved her. When her own parents abandoned her, Sister took her in and cared for her.

"It is God who cares for you," Sister had told her. "He is the one who protects us and cares for us."

Kioni thought of the young girls at the orphanage. Right now they would be gathered around the computer to watch her race—their faces intense, staring at the screen, their bodies jostling for a better position to see.

Mile twenty. Only six miles to go.

"Kioni, go, my girl. Go, Kenya! Go, Africa!" It was Sister Immaculata waving her cane.

In Africa this would be the turn to Runo's family farm. In her mind Kioni could see the gate. It was there that she had told Runo. It was there that the decision had been made. It was not fair to separate him from his parents. She had told him that she could not marry him.

The day before she'd left for Italy, she had told him. She had dressed carefully in the colors of Kenya, then oiled and prepared her hair. She had walked to Runo's family's farm and waited by the gate until Runo came home with his sheep.

"What is it?" he asked, concern in the lines of his forehead.

"I cannot marry you."

"You are sure?"

"I am. I cannot marry you with your parents not approving."

Her heart ached with pain, but it was right.

"You are braver than that."

"I am only an orphan. I have nothing to give."

"You have you, Kioni."

"I am not enough . . . for you."

She remembered the way he had looked at her as she left, standing at the gate as he'd watched her walk away down the path. She could not help but look back once, then twice, then a final time. He stood tall and straight. He looked at her with love, and her heart broke as she made the final turn away from Runo.

She had made the decision.

Now, only two days later in Italy, Kioni's legs and arms pumped the final miles. These miles were the most difficult, requiring total concentration. The smallest mistake could make the difference in the race. Pushing too hard could drain the energy. Lagging behind could give an opponent an advantage that could not be overcome. God would have to be with her now.

Mile twenty-three. It was this mile at home on the path where the impact of her decision had washed over her, and she began to weep as she walked alone toward the orphanage. She might be like Sister and not ever marry. But she loved Runo, and the idea of not being with him was painful.

Mile twenty-four. Concentrate.

The pavement was hard and the road under her feet

hot. The crowd was beginning to thicken here, and they cheered her on. The German was close and pulling closer.

Three more miles.

At mile twenty-four in Africa the path splits—one path goes up to the mountains, the other down to the orphanage. Kioni had stopped there for a moment on her long walk away from Runo. She remembered the pain she had felt as she'd looked at the two paths and accepted her choice.

The German. A sudden movement behind Kioni brought her back to Rome and the race. The German was inching closer to make her move. Kioni remembered the story of Gilda grabbing for the opponent's elbow. Out of the corner of her eye she saw Gilda's hand dart forward. Kioni edged left, not missing a step.

She heard a snort from Gilda. Again Gilda's hand shot forward. Again Kioni sprang left. Finally, Gilda made one last lunge. Kioni thought of the rod of God protecting her, and she sprang left one last time. Gilda stumbled, not enough to fall, but enough to lose several steps. She could not catch Kioni now. Kioni used the last of her energy in the sprint of the final two miles.

Mile twenty-five.

Kioni smiled. Mile twenty-five was her favorite mile. It was the place in Africa where the view of the evening sunset broke the sky—the place where Runo had caught up to her on her way back to the orphanage.

"Kioni," he had called, and she'd turned. She saw him standing there against the sun, and she knew she could never leave him twice.

"I will keep asking you until you say yes," he said.

She fell into his arms.

Mile twenty-six. The final mile of her path in Africa, the mile where Runo walked her home and asked Sister for her hand in marriage.

Twenty young girls had run out from the house and fields and gathered around as Runo told Sister, "I want to marry this woman."

"Your parents?"

Runo stood tall. "It is possible they will understand, or possible they will not."

Sister nodded.

"God will be our father," he said, then extending his arms to the young girls, "and these will be our sheep."

"Yes," Sister said.

The cheers of the young girls echoed in Kioni's mind, and she could still see them as they fell on Runo and Kioni, hugging and laughing and crying.

In a flash, the memories of the cheers of the girls were replaced by the cheers of the crowd at the finish line in Rome.

Kioni's chest broke the ribbon. Sister grabbed her and jumped up and down. "My girl, you won! You won for Kenya! You did it!"

Kioni grabbed the flag that Sister handed her and waved it at the cheering crowd.

Then a small Italian boy pushed his way through the crowd.

"You won."

"Yes, and your paper helped me." Kioni pulled the paper out of her pocket and handed it to the boy.

"What about an autograph?"

"I have something even better." Kioni got a pen from Sister and scribbled an autograph onto a small Kenyan flag.

The boy's face lit up, and he smiled before disappearing into the crowd with the paper and his flag.

"We will go home with our prize," Sister yelled above the cheers. "We will bring the prize money home to our girls!"

Kioni raised her hands in prayer. "God is my shepherd! He has protected me."

"Yes," said Sister. "Now let us go home to your husband."

"Yes," Kioni echoed. The sound of the word was unfamiliar on her lips, but so wonderful. "My husband."

CHAPTER

ten

---

*You prepare a table before me
in the presence of my enemies*

---

*L*OU LIBERATORE stood in the olive groves where he'd always found comfort. Today there was none. He looked beyond the Gulf of Naples to the Mediterranean Sea. The deep blues that in the past gave him peace now left him empty. The sun was beginning to rise, filtering light through the branches of the trees that he loved.

He ran his hands along the olive branches, branches that until Wednesday he'd thought were his and Frankie's, free and clear. When he looked at his hands, worn and callused, he saw his grandfather's hands and his father's hands—hands that had worked the groves for generations. He was glad that his grandfather was not here to see them lose the groves. He closed his eyes, and childhood images flooded his mind.

He and his brother Frankie moving from branch to branch, cupping their hands and stripping the stems, feeling a dozen or so of the smooth olives fall loosely into their fingers. Their grandfather was a purist when it came to harvesting the olives. While others had already moved to nets and bamboo canes, Grandfather Luca still insisted on hand stripping. By the end of the week their hands were as rough as the hessian bags where they dumped the olives.

Lou opened his eyes. He didn't want to think about

Frankie. They had been so close as children and even as adults, but two days ago things had changed.

"What's wrong?" Maria had asked when she'd found him holding the letter, standing like a marble statue in the kitchen.

At first he couldn't speak. He just stared at the notice from the bank.

"Lou, what's wrong?"

"The groves. Frankie . . ." was all he could say.

The paper from the bank was heavy in his hand, the words inconceivable.

Maria took the paper from him and read the words silently. Hard words like *lien* and *collateral* and *forfeiture*. Then, without speaking, she wrapped her arms around him, and they stood together in the kitchen, holding each other up.

"We'll be all right, Lou," Maria said. "We'll be all right."

Lou was not so sure.

The groves were not only their support, but their lives. They had raised their girls here, just as they had raised the additional small olive trees that they'd planted. As Lou walked through the orchard, he knew every tree. There would be no starting over. The groves had been cared for and nurtured for years. The gentle summer breezes coming up from the sea had made the trees grow thick and wide. The cold, strong winds of the winter coming down from the mountains had made them strong, sending deep roots down into the fertile volcanic earth.

Now, because of Frankie, all was lost.

Lou had thought of nothing else since. He felt

betrayed. An enemy betrayed you at the deepest level, not your brother. An enemy lied and stole from you, not your brother. An enemy destroyed you and your family, not your brother. Frankie, his brother, had done all those things. Now Frankie was about as close to an enemy as you could get and still be family—*famiglia*.

Lou left the grove and headed slowly down the path toward town. His shoulders stooped, more from disappointment than his fifty years. He didn't want to go to town. He didn't know whom he might meet that would know about the bank and the foreclosure.

As he passed each person on the small dirt road, he tipped his hat, like always. They nodded back, like always. Everything seemed the same on the outside, but inside he was writhing in pain and confusion.

He'd not left the house or the groves since the letter had come from the bank. Maria had asked him to pick up bread for tonight's dinner. She was tired of him pacing around the house, muttering to himself. Maria was not a woman to say no to. Tonight's dinner. His throat tightened as he thought about it.

The whole family was gathering for dinner. His daughters and their families, Uncle Dino and Aunt Teresa, the cousins. Everyone would be there, everyone except for Frankie. Lou could not imagine sitting at the same table with Frankie, not after what Frankie had done.

Tony Ricci was pulling hot loaves from the oven as Lou walked in.

"Lou, come in. Fresh bread, just for the Liberatores. You're practically family."

"Thanks, Tony. Our Grandfather Luca loved your papa's bread. Two loaves for tonight."

"Ah, big dinner?"

"Yeah."

"The whole family coming?"

Lou didn't answer. It would be everyone except Frankie.

Lou wondered if Tony knew. Had he heard about Frankie's debt? How he'd been slowly borrowing against the groves? How he'd traveled to Naples where his actions wouldn't get back to Lou or anyone else in the Sorrento area?

"That Frankie, he makes my heart laugh," Tony said.

Apparently Tony didn't know. Or perhaps he was just being nice—that would be like him.

"I need some wrapping paper!" Tony called to the back of the store. "I can't very well give Lou his bread naked." He laughed.

A young boy hurried out from the back with a single piece of paper.

"Here, Grandpa Tony, you can use this."

Tony took the paper. "A fine piece of paper. Go in the back and get me some extra paper from Grandma."

The boy hurried off.

"Alberto's such a good boy," Tony said. "He's our grandson, come from Rome to visit."

The boy rushed back with more paper. Tony wrapped the first loaf and started on the second. Then he noticed the writing.

"This paper has English on it, Alberto. Where did you get it?"

"From a girl in Rome. I was going to use it for an autograph, but the runner gave me a flag instead."

"You don't want to keep this paper?"

The boy shook his head. He pulled a small Kenyan flag from his pocket and waved it proudly. "I got this." He pointed to the autograph sprawled across the big red band in the middle.

"Very nice," Tony said. "Lou, I will leave the special English paper in with your bread, like a fortune cookie. Later you can tell me what it said."

Lou smiled. "I need a special message."

Tony handed him the loaves. "Give Frankie a hug for me."

There would be no hugs for Frankie. He was not invited to dinner. As far as Lou was concerned, he would never have dinner with Frankie again.

Lou began the climb up the winding road to his house in the hills.

How could Frankie do it? His father, grandfather, and great-grandfather had owned the same grove for moe than a hundred years. Lou looked at the olive groves that ranged the hillside. Great-grandfather Luca started with only a hundred trees. Lou's grandfather and father, also named Luca, had maintained the hundred. But when Lou and Frankie took over, Lou ran the business and started slowly buying up the surrounding groves. Now they had more than a thousand trees, or perhaps it was more accurate to say that now the bank had the trees.

In the distance Mount Vesuvius loomed large. Lou eyed the now dormant volcano. He felt like he could explode in the same way the mountain had so many years ago, spewing burning ash everywhere. He wanted to spew burning ash all over Frankie.

When Lou entered the house, the smell of Maria's osso buco almost made him forget his trouble. The care that she took in the sauce was the secret. The homegrown tomatoes and carrots from the backyard—they had been grown there for generations. And the garlic and parsley, always fresh. And that touch of lemon. Maria was simmering the sauce when he walked in. Time was what it took—time for the best things, like sauce and olives.

Lou tossed the loaves of bread onto the kitchen table.

As they rolled away, he saw the small piece of paper that Tony's grandson had gotten in Rome—Lou's "fortune cookie" tucked into the wrapping. Lou picked it up. He had taken English as a child and done pretty well. He slumped into a kitchen chair to read.

"Psalm 23," he said out loud. He slapped the paper with his hand. "I know this. It's from the Bible."

Lou continued reading, then suddenly stopped.

He read out loud, "'You prepare a table before me in the presence of my enemies!'" He threw his head back and laughed. "Ha! That is one spicy meatball."

"What's so funny?" Maria asked as she pushed past him to the oven. She pulled open the door and eyed the contents.

"It's the twenty-third psalm. It's the part about being in the presence of my enemies . . . and it made me think . . ."

Maria eyed him. "Frankie's still *famiglia*. He's not your

enemy. He's just . . . he's just Frankie. He's the same as he was when he was fifteen. Remember when he rode that mule through the middle of the Pascucci wedding parade? I tell you, no one in the town's forgotten it! And when he walked across the field in his white confirmation suit and got cow manure all over the legs?"

"Some things are funny when you're fifteen," said Lou. "This is not funny."

"True," she said, closing the oven.

She paused, then her face lit up with another story. "Remember when he was an altar boy and wore sandals?"

"Father D'Agostino just about had a fit," Lou said, smiling.

He remembered walking down the aisle that day side by side with Frankie, all dressed in their robes, every hair slicked into place. He had looked over and seen Frankie in sandals instead of the shiny, black Sunday shoes that were crimping his own feet. Lou smiled.

"And he told the priest that Jesus wore sandals," Lou said. Maria and Lou were both chuckling. Then Lou caught himself and frowned.

"This is different. This affects the family, the generations."

Maria wrapped her arms around him. Her voice softened. "It's not too late to invite Frankie for dinner."

Lou buried his head in his hands. "But think of the shame he brings to the family. The *famiglia.*" He circled his arms in the air for emphasis.

Maria put her hands on Lou's shoulders and rubbed them gently.

"The sun is still shining, and the groves are still producing."

He smiled at the recitation of the phrase she always used in times of trouble. He patted her hands.

This business with Frankie shouldn't have been a surprise. The way they had set up the groves, both brothers had control and could act independently; that included the right to borrow against the groves. At the time it never occurred to Lou that either of them would do that without consulting the other.

Lou sighed. "I just can't. I can't face him now."

"I understand. It was a terrible thing that he did."

Lou thumbed through the small stack of mail that he had picked up in the town. He began to open the envelopes, looking at the letters inside. The orders had been coming in regularly. The groves had developed a reputation, and Liberatore Olive Oil meant something to people all over the world. Who would make the olive oil now?

He opened the letters.

"Two from France."

"Good," Maria called from the stove.

"Another order from China. That's the third this year. And this order is for seventy-two bottles."

Maria brushed back her black curls. "See. The Liberatores are not done yet."

"I'm not so sure," Lou said.

Maria was in motion. "The dinner is done for now. Let's get the orders out right away. I'll go down to check on the packing."

She wiped her hands on her flowered apron and

pulled it off, then began to gather papers from around the room to pack the bottles.

"The sooner the shipment, the sooner the payment. Help me out and set the table for tonight. Will you, Lou?"

After she left, Lou sat for a moment, looking out the window. Usually he loved to set the table. Each dish and decoration had meaning for the family.

He got up and moved to the dining room. He rubbed his hand over the olive-wood table that Grandfather Luca had made. How many meals had he eaten at this table, covered by the white linen tablecloth, now draped over a chair and carefully ironed by Maria? He spread the cloth and touched the fine linen. The white embroidered flowers on the cloth were stitched by his aunts for his mother's wedding. *Famiglia.*

He prepares a table before me in the presence of my enemies.

Why would that verse come to him today? Why would God even want people to eat with their enemies?

Lou opened the china cabinet door. He pulled out the candlesticks that belonged to his grandmother. Those same candles lit the table for every meal he and Frankie had shared with Grandfather Luca when they were little. Grandfather Luca had lit the candles and said, "The light of the world." Lou remembered the glow of the candles and Frankie's huge, dark eyes staring as Grandfather told stories by the candlelight— always stories of the family.

"Nothing stops the Liberatores," Grandfather would say as he told of how their ancestors fought in the war to protect the land.

"Nothing stops the Liberatores," he would say after telling the story of the fire that destroyed half the olive trees when he was a boy.

Lou got the olive oil from the shelf. The family crest on the bottle was embossed in gold. It was a bottle from last year's harvest. He thought about those olives, poured into the press and then crushed. He felt crushed now, crushed between the bank and his family legacy. He thought about the trees growing wide and lush in the good times and strong and rooted in the harsh winter.

"Nothing stops the Liberatores," Lou said to Grandfather's empty chair. He set the olive oil on a saucer in the middle of the table.

He set out each of his grandmother's linen napkins and arranged her silverware at each place, in the order that Maria liked. He put out the salt and pepper shakers that had been in the family for as long as he could remember. When the table was set, he sat down in his place. He imagined each person at the table. Frankie's usual place looked empty without a place setting. But that was Frankie's doing.

Tomorrow Lou would travel to Naples and meet with the bankers. He would see what they would do, even though it might not be enough. Decisions would be made tomorrow. But today a table was set.

He remembered playing in the groves with Frankie. They were inseparable. Suddenly he wished his family didn't mean so much. Nowadays, the young people didn't seem to worry about family. *Famiglia* wasn't important. They left their small towns and headed off to the larger cities with what seemed like no thought at all about the fact that they were leaving their families behind.

How much he had loved his only brother, Frankie. Frankie had been there for him. The night before he was to marry Maria, he had gotten cold feet, and Frankie had talked him through it.

"Lou," he had said, those big eyes staring him through. "Take a chance this time. For once in your life, take a chance."

If Frankie hadn't pushed, Lou might not have gotten married. What he would have missed without Maria. He would have missed so much without Frankie and his "chances."

Lou walked back into the kitchen and brought out Tony's bread and placed it in the middle of the table, then pulled a bottle of wine from the hutch and set it beside the bread.

Suddenly he remembered Grandfather Luca holding up the bread and the wine and saying, "Bread and wine— ordinary stuff, boys—but in church, it's special. It is the body of the Lord, and His blood. His mercy to us."

Lou saw his rosary hanging on the peg by the door to the hallway. He went over and gently pulled it into his hands. He remembered praying through the beads as a boy. God had been at work in the Liberatores for a long time. Grandfather Luca certainly testified to that. He knew every prayer in the catechism, and he had encouraged Lou and Frankie to hold tight to the prayers.

Lou and Frankie had memorized everything together—the Apostles' Creed, The Hail Mary, the Glory

Be, the Our Father. And, the twenty-third psalm, in Latin, no less.

Lou smiled as he thought of two little boys saying the psalm, not having any idea what it meant to dine with an enemy. He touched the back of Frankie's chair.

He prepares a table before me in the presence of my enemies.

Lou stood facing the newly set table. He had carefully set the table piece by piece. Hadn't God carefully set the table, too, piece by piece—making Lou ready for this time? He looked at the empty chairs.

God had given Lou Maria to love him and to help him learn how to love. God had given them the girls, three beautiful daughters who had married and moved out, but not before turning his hair gray. They had taught him patience. And God had given him a brother, Frankie. So, what was Lou learning now? Maybe faith. That God had a plan for them. Maybe forgiveness. Someday.

Lou looked at the large wooden table that had been in their family for generations. Tonight they would all gather around this table. They would drink from the glasses of their great-grandfather. They would look at one another over the bread and wine—symbols of the eternal life they would someday share together.

They had had years together, simmering like Maria's tomato sauce, aging like the olive trees. Thousands of meals had been eaten at this very table, and time had done its work on the family, knitting them together, bonding them for good times and bad.

Maria came and stood beside him.

"It's beautiful, Lou."

She took his hand, and they stood silently for a moment, looking at the prepared table. Holding Maria's hand, reflecting on God's goodness, Lou felt bigger, stronger. He drew in a deep breath and let it out.

"He prepares a table before me," Lou said, "in the presence of my enemies."

"Yes," she said. "He does."

Lou's eyes filled with unshed tears. "Whatever he has done, he is still my brother. Whatever happens, we will face it with God and family, together. Okay, Maria. I'll set a place for Frankie."

CHAPTER

Eleven

You anoint my head with oil

OEY SAT ON THE BUS with all her worldly possessions close by, packed into a red, white, and blue rice bag and her well-worn backpack, a gift from her grandfather when she was in grade school. The threshold of a new life was fast approaching. She clutched her bags as the bus crawled through the narrow, congested streets of Chongqing.

It was six p.m., and people poured from the office buildings onto the sidewalks. Chongqing was always busy; after all, it was the biggest city in the world, thirty-two million strong. And at this hour it seemed like all thirty-two million were in the streets.

The man beside her shifted in his seat. She played her favorite game—imagine what people are doing. The man's eyes moved nervously, and his hands clutched a black bag tightly. *Robber.* She smiled at her active imagination. *Making a getaway . . . on this slow bus? Not a very good robber.*

There was a young woman dressed in a cocktail dress, a black silk wrap draped around her shoulders. *She's meeting a man,* Zoey decided. *She's getting engaged tonight.* The woman smiled at Zoey, and Zoey lowered her eyes.

The man across from her, wearing the dusty blue clothes of the village, was probably a farmer. He reminded her of her grandfather, and she knew what he was thinking about. *Sheep.* At least that's what her grandfather would be thinking of, always sheep. She felt a pang of pain as she remembered saying good-bye to him. He had been the hardest to leave. Her fingers unconsciously played with the fabric of the backpack he'd given her those many years ago.

When she was little, she had followed him everywhere, like the sheep he raised. They would sit together in the pastures and look up at the clouds.

"What is that, YeYe?" she would ask, pointing at a puffy white cloud.

"Sheep," he would answer.

"And that one?"

"Sheep."

She would giggle. He had seemed like a giant. Now, as she'd left him, he'd seemed so small.

"We are all sheep," he would say, and she would giggle.

"We are not sheep," she would tell him, shaking her tiny finger to scold him. "We are people."

"Sheep. People. It's all the same," he would say.

"Where are you going?" the woman beside her asked, looking at her bags.

"Los Angeles in the United States."

As she said the words, she felt fear rise. She had never been to the United States, and she only knew one person who had. It was Chan from the lab. He had done a fellowship there. He didn't talk much about it. He spent more time talking about the flight over and all the air turbulence. She had never flown on an airplane, either, and now she was planning to fly more than fifteen hours across the ocean. She pushed the thought from her mind.

It was exciting in a way, but scary, too.

She leaned her forehead against the cool window of the bus and watched the people outside, hurrying along the street with purpose. They all seemed so confident, while she felt anything but confident.

She was caught between her past and her future.

Her small dormitory room was empty now, and she was headed to Wang's apartment where three students from her medical class were meeting for dinner. She would spend the night with her friends Shi and Shu, then tomorrow she was off to her future in the United States. Her friends were rejoicing for her. She shivered at the thought.

Tonight they would celebrate their last night together. It was Italian night, and Wang would bring the wine. Shu and Shi would make the pasta and marinara sauce. Zoey was to bring the bread and oil. She had the bread and was on her way to pick up the oil.

She had known Wang since they were children. His father was the cobbler in their village. She could still see Wang in the shop, sitting on a bench beside his father, helping hammer soles onto shoes and pedaling the sewing machine while his father carefully stitched the seams.

When she was a baby, her father had left to work in the mines. YeYe was more of a father to her. She grew up following him like his sheep. Every fall they would shear the sheep. It was like magic, as they clipped away the dank and dirty wool and the new, soft, pure-white wool became exposed. She would laugh at the thin-boned bodies that emerged from beneath the mounds of dirty wool. The memories made her smile.

Zoey hopped off the bus with her bags and entered the import store.

"I'm looking for olive oil," she said. "It is for a dinner, so I want something special."

"This just arrived from Italy."

The woman held out a small box for Zoey to see. The bottle was in an individual carton, nestled safely in a bed of wrapping paper. Zoey could see the price. It was not quite as bad as she expected. She thought of her grandfather back in Xichang. He would have been horrified at the thought of fifty yuan for a bottle of oil. They paid half that for two gallons of soy oil, which lasted close to a month. But she was in Chongqing, and that's what things cost.

Besides, these friends were like brothers and sisters to her, at least what she thought brothers and sisters might be like. None of them actually had brothers or sisters.

"Is it good to dip Italian bread in?" Zoey asked.

"Oh yes. This is Liberatore Olive Oil—the best." The lady pointed to the gold label. "It comes from Sorrento, Italy, made by a family of generations of olive growers."

"I'll take it."

As Zoey handed the lady the money, she thought of all the people back in the village who were sacrificing for her to go to school—not just her grandfather, but their neighbors and the town leaders. They had all contributed to her education. She felt a tightness in her chest. Even today she had contemplated not going. Tomorrow morning, instead of going to the airport, she had imagined herself catching the bus. She could be back with YeYe in just a few hours. She would run through the pasture, past the sheep, straight to him. But everyone in the village would be disappointed. She could not let them down. She wanted them to be proud. She had to go to the United States. She would miss China, and her village, and YeYe, and the sheep, but she couldn't think about that now. Tonight was a happy night, dinner with her friends.

It was Shi and Shu's idea to have Italian night. They were good friends and so full of fun and ideas. They embraced the whole world and were always interested in other countries. It was funny that they were the ones staying in China while she was the one leaving to go so far away.

Zoey hurried along the busy sidewalk toward Wang's apartment. She loved the bustle of the city, so different from the village. She loved the village, too. Everything was so clean—the air, the green pastures of sheep. The thought of going back to the village was appealing, but she had been selected through a rigorous process and offered the opportunity to work in a major research university in the United States.

Would she be like the newly shorn sheep? All her traditions and memories clipped away? She could not even imagine it. She thought again about backing out and catching the bus home. *No.* Everyone expected her to go to the United States and to do well. She could never let them down after they'd done so much for her.

Zoey hurried up the stairs to Wang's apartment and

was soon enveloped in the hugs of her friends. The chatter and happy preparation for the meal took her mind off tomorrow and the flight and the beginning of her new life.

"Did you get the oil?" Wang asked.

"Yes."

Shi and Shu were boiling water in the kitchen.

"I got the spaghetti noodles," Shi said.

"And I got the marinara sauce," Shu added.

The girls were both from Qinghai province but different villages. They were going back to work in a hospital near their villages, so they would be starting their new jobs together. Wang was staying in Chongqing at the hospital they had trained in, so he would know lots of people there. Zoey was the only one venturing out alone. She would be flying to LA—alone. Beginning her residency—alone. Living in a one-room apartment—alone. She had never been so alone before.

As Zoey pulled the bottle of olive oil from the box, she noticed that one of the papers protecting the bottle looked different. Most of the wrapping was plain white, but this paper had handwriting on it. She pulled it out.

"What's that?" Wang asked.

"A paper, written in English."

"Isn't the oil from Italy?"

"Yes, but the paper is definitely English."

"Read it," Shu said, stirring the sauce.

Wang peered over Zoey's shoulder as she read.

"Okay. 'The Shepherd's Song. Psalm 23. The Lord is my shepherd; I shall not want . . .'"

Zoey read the entire psalm aloud.

"That's from the Christian Bible, I think," Shi said.

"Yes," Shu said. "I've heard it before, in my grandmother's house church."

Shi said, "I like the part about the green pastures and still waters. It reminds me of the villages in my province."

Shu nodded. "Yes, I am so glad we are returning to Qinghai, to the beautiful green pastures and clean air." She tossed the noodles into the boiling water.

Zoey said, "You are so lucky to be going together. I wish someone was going with me to the United States."

Wang took the paper and read, "'*He anoints my head with oil.*' I wonder what that means."

"Oil makes everything better!" Shi said, dipping a piece of bread in the oil and putting it into her mouth.

Wang also dipped a piece of bread in the oil and placed it in his mouth. He closed his eyes and sighed with pleasure.

"When I think of oil," Wang said, "I remember pot stickers! My mother frying pot stickers every night. Hmm, the crispness."

"You *would* think of food!" Zoey said.

"Also," said Wang, "I think of stir-fry!"

"Food again!" Shi rolled her eyes.

"Of course. I live to eat. You don't get this by avoiding food." He grabbed a small roll of fat from his abdomen.

They laughed.

Shu said, "When I think of oil, I think of eucalyptus oil. For hundreds of years my ancestors used it for healing.

When I go home, I am going to discover its secrets and become a famous doctor. Everyone will admire me, and I will be on the cover of many magazines. I might even win the Nobel Prize for medicine." She took a bow, and they all laughed.

"When I was a girl," Shi began, "I wanted beautiful hair, like this very popular girl in my village. Every night my mother would caress my hair with palm oil scented with lavender. I can still smell the oil." Shi stopped, her eyes filled with tears.

They were all silent for a minute.

"I'll brush your hair," Shu said. They laughed and hugged each other.

Wang pulled out his phone and clicked on his dictionary. He said, "'Anoint' means 'to apply oil.'"

"When I think of applying oil," Zoey said, "I remember my yeye. He took such good care of his sheep. He poured oil over their heads, rubbing it around their noses and eyes to protect them from the flies and gnats."

Zoey thought about how gentle his hands were as he rubbed the oil into the soft wool and on the black noses.

Wang nodded. "Your grandfather had healthy sheep; I remember they were the best-looking sheep around. Not like Mr. Chang's sheep."

Zoey thought of Mr. Chang's sheep in the next pasture with their infected skin and dripping noses. Some of them had gone crazy from insects laying eggs in the soft black membranes of their noses. The ewes had stopped giving milk, and the lambs had stopped growing.

YeYe's protection had kept his sheep healthy and

well. If only he could do the same for her—anoint her with oil to bring protection as she traveled to the United States, as she met new people and learned new customs.

How happy YeYe's sheep were after the anointing. They would press so close to him, their shepherd, knowing that he would provide what they needed and protect them. Who would protect her?

"I like the idea of protection," Wang said. "In a city as big as Chongqing, I need protection."

"I want protection from crashing airplanes," Zoey said.

They laughed.

"One time," Shu said, "at my grandmother's home church, they used oil in a kind of ceremony. They dipped a finger into the oil and then touched the forehead of a man; then they said, 'God be with you, amen.' He was going to be a minister."

Wang was already typing on his phone.

"'Amen' means 'it is so,'" he said.

"'God be with you; it is so,'" Zoey said. "Amen." Zoey repeated the foreign-sounding word. She thought about the anointing of the man at the church service and how comforting it would be to have God with her: on that plane, in LA . . . at her job.

The table was soon filled with the familiar laughter of the friends as they shared stories and memories of their time together. After the meal they sat together one last time.

The excitement of going to new places faded, and

sadness set in as they thought about no longer seeing one another.

They looked at the paper lying in the middle of the table beside the oil.

"Do you think God would go with us? And protect us?" Zoey asked. She thought about the house church and this idea of a God who anoints his followers, like YeYe anointed the sheep.

They were quiet for a minute, each pondering the future.

Then Shu said, "Here." She dipped her finger in the oil. She leaned forward and pressed her finger to Zoey's forehead. The oil was warm, the touch gentle. Zoey closed her eyes and imagined YeYe's finger touching her . . . or was it the finger of God?

She was strangely filled with peace and even a certainty that God was with her.

She dipped her finger in the oil and touched Wang's forehead.

"Remember this night," she said. "God go with you."

Wang smiled. He touched the oil and then pressed his finger first on Shi's forehead, then Shu's.

The candles glowed. The silence wrapped around them like a blanket, and a comfortable peace settled on them as they sat together.

Finally Zoey broke the silence in a voice that was more of a whisper. "He anoints my head with oil."

The four responded together: "Amen."

MORNING CAME. Zoey sat in the terminal, waiting for her flight. Her bags were checked; she had passed through security and had an hour to wait before boarding. She looked around at all the people traveling and wondered about each one. The man beside her was perfectly dressed and carefully groomed. *He must be on his way to meet the president,* she thought, and smiled.

An older woman sat with her hands folded. Around her were several bags and packages. *She's definitely one of those cool American CIA agents,* Zoey thought, covering her smile. *She's in disguise for a secret mission.*

And what would they think, she wondered, if they looked at her? A young girl alone—but she was not alone.

She pulled the psalm out of her bag and reread the words. *You anoint my head with oil.* Memories of the dinner came back and the great time she had had with her friends. She touched her forehead where Shu had anointed her with the oil.

YeYe would not be taking care of her now, or possibly ever again. But she had a different shepherd. One who would protect and feed her and comfort her.

"Flight 234, now boarding for Los Angeles."

She gathered her things quickly and made her way to the gate. Left on the seat was the psalm, forgotten in her excitement to board. But the words were a part of her now, giving her confidence and speaking to her heart of a very real God, who even cared for her.

She paused for a moment to look outside the big glass windows at the plane that would take her to her future. The sky was bright blue; white puffy clouds floated above.

"*Sheep*," she could almost hear YeYe saying. "*Sheep. People. We are all the same.*"

"Now boarding, flight 234 to Los Angeles."

Zoey smiled and turned toward the plane. YeYe could not go with her, but her shepherd God could go anywhere. And He would protect her, too. After all, that's what it promised in the psalm.

You anoint my head with oil.

She stepped forward toward the plane and into her future with a newfound confidence she had never known.

CHAPTER

twelve

My cup overflows

---

*A*H, FIRST CLASS."

Roland Shelby was tilting back in his first-class airplane seat, filled with the warmth of wealth and success, when his worst nightmare came true. Her name was Judy.

It had been a great trip. He had sealed the Wilson-Chamberlain deal in Chongqing. It looked like it was going to be a great flight home. The first leg to LA had been easy, and now on the final leg to New York the seat beside him was empty. That was the great thing about first class; you were away from the riffraff. No one to bother you. Time to contemplate the next deal. That's when he heard the voice beside him.

"Excuse me, young man. I believe I'm in that seat."

She was carrying no less than four bags. *What happened to the two carry-on policy?* He rose and stepped into the aisle to let her pass.

She squeezed past his seat and collapsed with a thud into hers.

"Let's see, now." She fumbled through the bags. "This one needs to go under the seat." She dropped one bag on the floor and pushed it under the seat in front of her. "And this one I'll keep here, then I can . . ."

Oh great, he thought, *she's going to give a running commentary on everything she does and every thought she has.*

My cup overflows

He looked around hopefully for an empty seat, an escape from Judy. All around he saw men in expensive suits, businesswomen in heels and perfectly coiffed hair, already typing on their computers or cell phones. Even the casual people wore expensive clothes. Every seat was taken.

She'd likely been upgraded because coach was full. Just his luck. He'd be stuck here beside her for five hours, all the way from Los Angeles to New York.

"Judy," she announced, extending an unwelcome hand.

"Roland." He shook her hand, but it was a very light handshake. He smiled as he thought of all the "power" handshakes he'd experienced in his life, each person trying to grip a little firmer, a little stronger—to show greater strength, power—to intimidate. He had even once considered getting a gym membership, just to strengthen his right arm for handshaking.

"Can I get you something to drink?" the flight attendant asked.

"Amstel Light in a cold mug." He'd need a beer for this flight.

"Hmmmm," Judy said. "Sweet tea?"

Roland did a double take. *What planet is she from?*

The words "sweet tea" took him back, way back to his grandmother's house in Georgia. Sweet tea. It made his mouth ache to think of the taste of sweet tea.

He took in her worn, embroidered sweater. Her small hat. *Brother.* He was flying halfway across the world with his grandmother!

The attendant was shaking her head no.

Roland rolled his eyes.

To stop further conversation, he pulled the stack of documents and financial magazines out of his briefcase. A folded piece of paper fell out onto his lap. It must have belonged to the Asian girl who'd sat beside him in the waiting area in Chongqing. They had both piled their things on the chair between them. Curious, he unfolded the paper and read.

The Lord is my shepherd; I shall not want.

That's right, he thought. *I don't want for anything.* He thought of his new BMW Z4 and how good it made him feel.

He continued to skim the psalm until he came to "my cup overflows." *Yes, my cup* does *overflow. My bonus this year will be double last year's. Overflowing!*

The attendant handed him his beer.

"My cup overflows," he said to Judy, lifting his beer glass to toast.

To his surprise, she laughed and returned the toast with her Diet Coke.

"Indeed," she said.

Roland tucked the paper into the seat pocket and leaned his head against the back of the seat as the plane taxied down the runway. The plane lifted off, and there was blessed silence until they reached cruising altitude.

For him, life was like a chessboard with one complicated move after another, and he always managed to win. He was drawn to deals like a moth to a flame. And he could sniff out the good ones. He could read people, too, so deals were easy. He smiled as he thought of the Wilson-Chamberlain deal and how he had spotted the slight squint in the eyes of the opponent at a crucial point in the negotiation . . . and how he'd moved in for the kill. *Ah. It felt good.*

"Do you have any children, Roland?" Judy interrupted his thoughts.

"I have a daughter."

"I have five children, and a wealth of family and friends, too. They are all coming."

"For what?"

"Thanksgiving. Isn't that why you're flying home?"

Roland shook his head. He hadn't realized it was Thanksgiving. He remembered the message from Sarah inviting him to dinner and cringed to think that he had never called her back. Thanksgiving was Thursday. He would be having dinner at the Fleur de Lis with his financial advisers. Tournedos of beef and béarnaise sauce—a good Cabernet.

"Roland, you reminded me of something important. My cup overflows."

"Mine does, too." Roland thought of the good Cabernet. "Especially when I can get some sleep," he added as a hint. He pulled out the eye cover that the airline provided and put it on.

He didn't want to hear about her cup overflowing. He liked his own cup, with a luxury car and a big house and first class and big business deals. He thought about his penthouse. He loved the way they treated him when he walked in the door.

"Good morning, Mr. Shelby." The doorman was

quick to open the door and stand at attention while he walked into the building.

"Good, Mr. Shelby." The attendant would hurry to press the button on the elevator. Now *that* was success. Not having to press your own elevator button.

Upstairs his place was spotless, expansive, immaculate. Gleaming granite and polished wood. No one to mess it up. It was empty most of the time. Sarah had her own place now, and he didn't have time for relationships.

He had done it. He had accomplished everything that he had set out to do in his life.

"Um." Judy again. "Um, excuse me." He lifted up one part of the eye shield and saw her rising.

"Can you excuse me? I need to, um, powder my nose."

Suddenly she was almost on his lap. He tried to help her over but didn't quite know where to touch. Mercifully, she finally made it to the aisle.

He straightened his glasses, which now hung sideways on his face. His tie was askew. He fixed the knot. He looked at her empty seat and shook his head. *Some people are satisfied with so little.* He was thankful that he appreciated the finer things in life. He sipped his beer and planned his evening. He would have the driver stop at The Browning Club. They had a great porterhouse steak on Wednesday nights. He looked down at his pile of potential deals. He could review those some more tonight.

Memories of the old house in Georgia crept into his thoughts. He cursed Judy under his breath. She had reminded him of the old days with her talk of sweet tea and

Thanksgiving, and now he was stuck with memories that he had avoided for so long.

Growing up, there had never been enough of anything—food, money, stuff. He remembered his mother trying to stretch the food at the end of each month, how he and his two brothers would often share one package of ramen noodles. They were always hungry. Thanksgiving was the only meal he remembered where he could eat all he wanted. He had vowed that he would never be hungry again.

He thought of his penthouse and the cook who prepared his meals. He rubbed the soft cashmere of his jacket sleeve and straightened his fine silk tie. Yes, he decided, his cup was overflowing, over and over. The past was the past.

"Excuse me."

Judy was back. Roland jumped up quickly to let her get to her seat. As she settled in, he closed his eyes to discourage conversation.

"Ta-da!" Judy interrupted his nap. Roland opened his eyes to find a small pastry on his seat-back tray.

"Pecan tassie!" Judy said, "Happy Turkey Day!"

Roland eyed the small tart. The buttery, flaky crust looked light. The filling glistened in sugary wonder, and crushed nuts rode atop.

It was so pedestrian. So old-fashioned. So . . . He looked at the flakiness of the crust. *So delicious looking.*

He popped it in his mouth.

He was overcome by the sensations exploding in his mouth—the butter, the hint of maple, the nuts, the filling. The taste of the tart swept him back to his grandmother's kitchen table, the only place he had ever been full.

"Mmmm," was all he could say. The taste of the tart had broken down something inside him, and he was six years old again.

"Mmmmm," he said again, running his tongue around his mouth to get every bit of sweetness.

"Mmmmmm," he said one more time, before he realized that the man across the aisle was looking at him.

He tried to concentrate on the financial sheets for the Wilson-Chamberlain deal, but he kept thinking about the tart. The idea of Thanksgiving brought back so many memories.

"You make that?" he asked.

She nodded. "I'm cooking the rest at my son's house. What a feast we will have." Her eyes took on a dreamy quality.

"My son thinks it's all about the turkey. He's bringing it, and he will be up at the crack of dawn to start cooking it. But it's not about the turkey."

Roland was nodding.

"It's the other stuff."

"Yes." He was amused that he was actually agreeing with her.

She handed him another tart. Crumbs fell down onto his silk tie, but he didn't notice.

"Mmmmm." He didn't care who heard him this time.

"You want to know how I make the gravy?"

"The gravy?" All his thoughts of béarnaise sauce and

tournedos of beef were suddenly gone, replaced by the thought of gravy—glistening, steaming, brown gravy.

"Thanksgiving is all about the gravy," Judy continued. "Now, first . . ."

"Giblet gravy?"

"Of course." She took a breath. "Now, first, you brown the flour. That's the secret. It removes all the moisture so you don't have lumps, and the gravy is silky smooth. You put half a cup of flour in a skillet, and stir it and shake the pan till it turns brown. Watch close, though; you could burn it. Then set it aside, and boil your giblets."

Roland was spellbound.

"When the turkey's done, you pour a cup of drippings into your browned flour in the skillet. It will sizzle, and you stir it into a paste. Mmmmmm, the smell of those drippings.

"Then you start adding your broth, one cup at a time, till you get six cups in. Then stir, and watch it thicken. Add salt and pepper, and it's the richest, creamiest, savoriest."

Roland closed his eyes. His mouth was watering. He was back at his grandmother's table. All he could think about was gravy.

"You know the best part of Thanksgiving food?" Judy asked.

Visions of turkey and dressing, cornbread and gravy filled his mind.

"Best is the leftovers."

"Oh yeah," he said, rubbing his hand together, "the leftovers."

"My grandkids can't even wait for the next day before they make a turkey sandwich. You ever heard of the moist maker?"

He shook his head, the papers forgotten. "Go on," he said.

"You make your sandwich with three slices of bread instead of two." She paused.

"Go on."

"One slice you soak in the leftover gravy."

His stomach growled.

"That slice goes in the middle—makes the sandwich moist. Then you put on your turkey slices, stuffing, cranberry sauce, a little mayo, and barbecue potato chips for crunch."

He thought of his empty Sub-Zero refrigerator, clean and gleaming. He hadn't had leftovers since he had left his wife.

They both leaned back in their seats, as though they'd just finished the Thanksgiving meal themselves. Roland closed his eyes. Time passed. Roland's mind drifted to business and his deals and his plans. But somehow his mind kept returning, like a homing pigeon, to food.

"Cranberry sauce with berries?" he asked. "Or jellied?"

"Both!" she answered.

He remembered the table, the turkey glistening, ready to be carved. The lima beans resting in their oval bowl, a pat of butter melting on top.

"Stuffing? Or dressing?" he asked.

"Both!"

Both! He loved both stuffing inside the bird and dressing, crunchy cornbread dressing in a casserole. He could see his grandmother's hands clasping two thick pot holders, bringing the dressing to the table.

"Rice? Or mashed potatoes?"

"Both!"

He remembered mashing the potato chunks with butter and dollops of sour cream.

He could hardly ask the next question.

"Pecan? Or pumpkin?"

"Pies! Oh pies," she said. "Pecan, sweet potato, chocolate cream pie, and vinegar pie. Like my mother used to say, 'gracious plenty.'"

He could hardly stand it.

The flight attendant placed a small oval dish containing a piece of dried chicken and some green beans in front of him. He took a bite, then pushed it aside.

Judy looked at him. "You sure must love Thanksgiving."

"I haven't had a Thanksgiving dinner in years," he said. "Never enough time."

"You know what's the real best thing about Thanksgiving?" she asked.

She had Roland's full attention now.

"The people. The people around the table."

Then Roland saw them. Unbidden, they came into his mind. His grandmother and grandfather. His mother and his little brother, wide-eyed at the bounty before them. His aunts and uncles. His father—the one time a year Roland saw him.

Suddenly Roland's eyes filled with tears. He coughed and pretended he had something in his throat.

"Coffee?" The flight attendant handed each of them a cup of coffee, and Roland held his.

Judy smiled. "Maybe you could join us for dinner?"

He looked at her. She was inviting him to Thanksgiving dinner.

"Oh, never mind," she said. "I know you are much too busy."

She smoothed out her sweater.

He thought about himself at her table surrounded by her family and her neighbors and her friends. He thought about the leftovers he would take home, her leftovers. *Her* cup overflowed.

The small airline coffee cup, now empty, rested in his hand.

He could have the finest food that money could buy. He could have the most expensive wine in the world. But *people*, that was different. People could not be bought.

"Tray tables up," the attendant reminded them.

The plane landed.

As they taxied to the terminal, Roland reached for his phone. He remembered the message earlier from Sarah: *Come by if you can. We are having a few friends over for Thanksgiving dinner, and we'd love to set a few more places.*

He looked at the phone. Why was it so easy to call the most powerful financial giants in the world but so hard to call one young woman? He took a deep breath and pushed her number.

"Sarah," he said.

"Dad?" She sounded surprised. "What's wrong?"

"I'm coming."

Silence.

He continued. "For dinner—for Thanksgiving."

Still nothing from the other end of the phone. *It's too late*, he thought, *too many years have gone by. Too many dinners have been missed.*

"It's okay, Sarah. I understand."

He found that he could not move.

The Lord is my shepherd, he thought, *but my cup is empty. God, please fill my cup.*

"Sarah?" he asked.

He heard a sniffle on the other end of the phone, and he realized that she was crying.

"I'm here, Dad."

"Can I come?" he asked.

"Yeah, Dad. I'd love for you to come."

His breath released in a long whoosh, and he was filled with a feeling of goodness that he had not felt for a long time—a gracious plenty that had nothing to do with food or things. It was the kind of overflowing that made leftovers.

Judy pulled a card out of one of her bags.

"Well, if you find you can come, here's my address."

Roland took the card and glanced at it.

"Judith Willingham Castleman."

He smiled. Judith Willingham Castleman was one of the wealthiest women in New York City. Her real estate holdings alone were massive.

As they taxied to the gate, Roland found himself pondering the overflowing cup. All the things he had thought were so valuable—business deals, possessions, wealth, Judy's real estate—didn't really make your cup overflow.

Simple words on a paper from God had pulled his life into perspective. And a simple "Yeah, Dad, you can come" had made his heart so full it seemed to overflow. His cup overflowed, and it had nothing to do with his possessions.

"Thanks, Judy," he said. "I'm having Thanksgiving with my daughter this year. My cup overflows."

"Gracious plenty?" Judy asked, looking at his contented smile.

"Yes," he said. "A gracious plenty."

CHAPTER

thirteen

---

*Surely goodness and mercy shall
follow me all the days of my life*

Little Bunny lived all alone in a lavender cave in the dark woods.

CORNELIA LOOKED at the sentence on her computer screen. Good start. She congratulated herself by eating a Hershey's Kiss. The first sentence of a book was the most satisfying to write. Actually, the first sentence was the only thing that she had written.

What next? Cornelia thought about her story. She felt Little Bunny's loneliness. Her own world had been shrinking and was now reduced to one room in Happy Acres Assisted Living.

The room hadn't turned out like she'd hoped. At her house she had decorated each room with such care. She had always loved the color lavender. *Each room needs a touch of lavender,* she had read once in the *Ladies' Home Journal,* so she had accented each room in her home with a touch of it. Now it seemed that all those accents had come with her, making her room into one big Easter basket of lavender.

Her possessions had been "downsized," too, reduced to the contents of one dresser, a small closet, and one desk. A few pictures lined the top of the dresser: her daughter, Tanya, in cap and gown, graduating from college—Carl with his arm around her, smiling as he always did. She thought they would always have each other. Now she was stuck here in this small room, alone like Little Bunny.

She turned away from Carl's picture. She was giving him the silent treatment. It was hard to give the silent treatment to someone who had passed, but if anyone could give the silent treatment, it was Cornelia.

The cursor on her screen blinked steadily as she thought. She shook her head, then turned back to her computer and continued typing:

> One day Little Bunny decided to see the world.
> Little Bunny stepped out of the cave into the open woods.
> Snip. Snap. A huge hawk swooped down and ate her up!!!

Cornelia added several more exclamation points. She chuckled at the story, then realized with horror that she had just eliminated her main character in the first paragraph. How could she? Quickly she pushed the delete button. She would never finish a story if she killed off her main character.

Her heart began beating rapidly in a funny, jumping rhythm, and she felt a slight pain in her chest. She took deep breaths. She did not want to end up in the infirmary. It was even more dreary than her lavender room.

Cornelia looked at the computer screen and felt guilt at her thoughts and the death of Little Bunny. She turned the computer off and unwrapped two more Hershey's Kisses. She needed a boost anyway. Her daughter, Tanya, was coming for dinner. She knew what Tanya wanted, and she wasn't ready to give it. Tanya wanted her to forgive Carl and stop giving him the silent treatment.

"Hey, Mom, we just landed." Tanya blew in with a burst of energy and efficiency. She was still in her flight attendant's uniform. She threw her coat across the bed and sat in one of the two armchairs in the room.

"Where were you this time?" Cornelia was amazed by her daughter's travels around the world, every day a different place. How could she and Carl, who had never left Martinsville, have raised this independent young woman?

"Los Angeles to New York, then a short hop home to Baltimore." Tanya emptied her pockets of peanuts and biscotti cookies, goodies that her mother loved. "And I brought you something else. I found this in one of the seat pockets in first class, and it looked like something you would like."

She handed her mother the folded paper. Cornelia took one look, saw the Bible verse, and pushed the paper across the desk. It was crumpled and old like her, and she didn't want to look at it.

Tanya had talked her into moving here—for the social life, she had said. Bingo and cha-cha lessons. Book clubs and movie nights. What would she do with cha-cha lessons? She might cha-cha her hip right out of joint.

"Have you written anything?" Tanya asked.

Cornelia didn't answer.

"Have you tried out the computer, like I showed you?"

Tanya had set up the computer last week.

Cornelia had always wanted to write a children's book. She had spent her life caring for children. How many books had she read backward with the pictures facing out toward the eager eyes of children? Miss Corn, they called her. Miss Corn could really read a story. She made the characters come to life, each with a different voice and style. How she loved story time. With books she could travel the world without ever leaving her own lavender armchair.

"Today we are going to Japan," she would tell the children, pulling out a picture book covered with girls in kimonos. Or, "We are going to the Wild West." Or Alaska.

Books were her own personal airline.

She longed to write her own stories, but when she tried, she just stared at the computer screen and nothing came. Or worse, she killed innocent animals.

"Nothing yet," she answered truthfully.

She had read that writer's block was simply fear. Maybe that was true. Certainly, the world had seemed safer when Carl was in it. He was her rock and kept her stable. As long as he was with her, she had felt that she could do anything.

"Ready for dinner?" Tanya asked, checking her hair in the mirror, not noticing her mother's anger.

Cornelia glanced into the mirror and shrugged. Another meal in the dining room. Another lonely night ahead. Didn't matter how she looked. Cornelia took her walker, and they began the slow walk to the dining hall.

"Hey, Miss June," Tanya called to June Banks.

"I don't know why you aren't friends with June," Tanya said. "She seems so sweet, always taking those prayer requests."

June waved back gamely from her post at the end of the hall, where she monitored the weekly gossip.

"Prayer requests? Or gossip opportunities?" Cornelia asked with a snort.

"Hey, Dr. Frank." Tanya waved at a man sitting in front of his room in a wheelchair.

"What about Frank? He has cute, twinkly eyes. He was a dentist. He's sweet."

"Sweet like a toothache," Cornelia said. "Last Tuesday morning everyone woke up with their dentures missing. Turned out Dr. Frank thought he was back at work and collected them all. Every last one. I'll keep my dentures safe, if you please."

Tanya laughed. "Okay. But there must be someone here you could like."

They picked up their trays and made their selections, chicken à la king over toast points.

They settled in at the table when Tanya began.

"Mom, I think you should go to the cemetery with me tomorrow."

"When did you get so bossy? I'm not of a mind to go. I'm still giving Carl the silent treatment."

"Mom, Daddy's dead," Tanya said. "You can't give the silent treatment to someone who is dead."

"Hmph. It *does* take some of the fun out of it."

"Maybe it's time to forgive him. He always hated the silent treatment."

Cornelia didn't answer. Carl *did* hate the silent treatment.

She remembered how he would beg her, "Corn, please. Not the silent treatment; anything but the silent treatment." All the while his crinkly eyes would be smiling, making her even madder.

"Here, Corn," he would say. "Just go ahead and hit me right here." He would point to his chin. "Just talk to me."

Cornelia started to smile thinking about it but caught herself. She turned her attention to the food and stopped the conversation.

"Okay, Mom," Tanya said as she hugged her good-bye. "Call me if you change your mind."

Cornelia hugged Tanya tight, hating to see her go, hating to be left alone—alone with Little Bunny in her lavender cave.

After Tanya left, Cornelia turned on her computer. She pulled the keyboard toward her and began.

> Little Bunny lived all alone in a lavender cave in
> the dark woods.

She was off to a good start this time. She thought about dinner and Tanya's urging her to see Carl. Why wouldn't people—Tanya, to be exact—just let her be?

She had always been known as a kind person, so different from the woman who gave her dead husband the silent treatment and murdered helpless bunnies in her imagination.

Cornelia turned to the document and typed.

Little Bunny peeped out.

She thought of all the possibilities for Little Bunny. There was a time in her life when anything seemed possible.

She thought of an eagle swooping down to devour Little Bunny. She thought of the dangers of raging streams that could sweep her away, of storms and lightning that could harm her.

She looked down at her hands, which were clasped in tight fists, like a boxer ready to punch. She turned to look out the window, her hands still clenched. Her heart had started its strange rhythm after the second ending of Little Bunny's life, but now it settled to a calmer, more steady pattern. She took a deep breath.

"I want to forgive you, Carl," she said to his picture, "but I can't."

"Please don't give me the silent treatment" His crinkly eyes looked out from the picture, bringing the words to mind.

She turned the picture to the wall. "I miss you," she said softly.

She picked up the paper that Tanya had found on the airplane. The loneliness of the room was closing in. At least the paper was something different. She unfolded it. It was an old psalm, one she had memorized as a child. She focused on the end—*Surely goodness and mercy shall follow me all the days of my life.* Was that true?

No, it was not true. It had been true in the early years. Goodness and mercy were woven into her life, like the stitching in a quilt she made for Tanya—but the stitching had begun to unravel. First Tanya left, heading out to the community college, then the job at the airlines, and the move to the city.

Then Carl left her. Not his body, but his mind. She was so afraid when Carl began to wander away. She still remembered the fear she'd felt the first time she had found him missing. It seemed impossible that he could have left without her knowing. She had run to each room, looking, searching, trying to find him, trying to think with his brain where he could have gone. But that was the problem; his brain was no longer there. He was silent.

The police had come quickly when she'd called. Neighbors had gathered at the edges of their yards to look and see what was going on. Later, Carl was found wandering up the interstate in his bathrobe and slippers. That was the beginning of the end, as she saw it now.

It was the beginning of the journey that would lead her to Happy Acres and lead him to the memory unit. She was surprised at how happy he was as soon as he was confined, how content he was with the smallness of his world, the smallness of a single room. But she had not been ready for the smallness. She had not been ready to see her world shrink, and shrink to this lavender cocoon. It wasn't fair.

She looked at the paper with the psalm again. It was well worn. Someone had carried it around a long time. And it was covered with stains. A little coffee on the edge, a smudge of green, a bit of red lipstick, and oil, too. Her creative mind began to imagine who might have caused those stains and what their lives were like. They were probably ordinary people, just like her. Cornelia looked more carefully at the pictures on her dresser. What a full and wonderful life she had experienced.

"What happened, Carl?" she said to the back of his picture. "Why did you leave me?"

She remembered the first words Carl had said to her, long ago after a school pep rally. "May I walk you home?" It seemed old-fashioned now, but it was so romantic at the time. She could still see him in his jeans and button-down shirt—hair cut short and always combed back, his coffee-brown face and deep-brown eyes framed by his wire-rimmed glasses.

"Oh, Carl," she said. "I wish you could see me home."

Memories came back, good memories. Camping with Carl and Tanya in Cloudland Canyon, the rain dripping into the tent and the laughter and squeals as they dodged the raindrops. Their big backyard barbecues with friends and neighbors and church family, Carl always at the grill, spatula in hand, wearing his silly chef hat that embarrassed her.

Goodness and mercy described her life up to this point. Life had been so good, so perfect. Going forward would be different.

She looked down at the paper.

The big question, she realized, was could she trust God with her future? She felt as helpless as Little Bunny.

"Goodness and mercy shall follow me," she read, and the words *follow me* stood out. For something to follow you, you had to be moving. God had given her Carl to walk with her through life. Now she needed to keep walking. She felt God saying, *"May I walk you home?"*

"Can I trust you, God?" she asked. "Can you be my rock?"

Other memories came back now. She had thought of her life with Carl as perfect, but it wasn't without trouble. There they were in the emergency room, holding Tanya as a baby, fever raging. Carl was praying. Later, the fever had turned. And there she was, sitting in the doctor's office, holding Carl's hand for her first bout with breast cancer. God's goodness and mercy had come every day as she and Carl had dealt with each frightening appointment in prayer.

There was goodness and mercy again when Carl lost his job at the factory. And yet again when they were down to their last can of food. They had walked through it all together. They had walked through it all with God.

She picked up Carl's picture and turned it around. The most painful memories returned—Carl looking at her with his blank eyes, silent.

"Why?" she said, weeping. Her tears fell on the glass of Carl's face and dropped down on the psalm in her lap. "Why did you give me the silent treatment?"

There. There it was. Worse than anything, anything that could possibly happen to her. Carl had forgotten her.

"God, please don't forget me, too," she said through the tears. "Please don't give me the silent treatment."

Her breath let out. Her heart slowed its rhythm. She held the picture tenderly, looking into the loving eyes of her husband. She placed him in his spot on the dresser.

She sat with the psalm and realized that God was speaking to her through the words on the crumpled paper. God promised her goodness and mercy *all* the days of her life. As she held the psalm, the anger drained from her mind, replaced by gratitude. God had not forgotten her. God was not giving her the silent treatment.

"Thank you, God," she said. "Thank you, Carl."

In the stillness of the lavender room she felt God's presence.

"Okay, God," she said. "I hear you."

In the lavender room she was not alone.

"Okay, God," she said finally. "You may walk me home."

Cornelia took a deep breath and blew it out. She looked at the blinking cursor. "You are one tough Little Bunny," she said to the screen, and she began to type.

> Little Bunny stepped out of the safety of the
> cave.

That felt right. Felt big. She didn't know what would happen next in her life, but she knew that God would be with her. When she turned off the computer, her own reflection looked back. She touched her wrinkled skin and patted her gray hair.

"You are one tough Bunny," she repeated to her reflection.

"Okay, Carl," she said to his picture. "The silent treatment is over."

She picked up the psalm and thought about what she could do with it.

Like me, she thought, *old and worn, and even a few stains, but not done yet. God is not finished with me.*

"Goodness and mercy shall follow me all the days of my life," she read. "All the days."

She would not act like her life was over just because it was different. She picked up the phone and called Tanya.

"I'm ready. I want to go see Carl tomorrow."

"Oh, Mom. I'll pick you up at ten."

————

CORNELIA SAT WAITING in the hall chair, hands folded, coat buttoned, Carl's favorite of her hats proudly atop her head.

Dr. Frank rolled by.

"How're your teeth doing?" Cornelia asked.

Dr. Frank looked thoughtful. "They will be ready next Tuesday."

Cornelia smiled, and Dr. Frank smiled back. June waved from down the hall.

"Going out?" she pumped for information.

Cornelia smiled again. Her smile muscles were getting a workout.

"Yes. Going to see my husband."

June looked surprised. Cornelia chuckled. *That will give her something for the prayer list.*

Tanya came in and hugged her mother. "You look great."

They walked slowly toward the door and into the bright morning outside. A little anxiety washed over Cornelia. "All the days," she whispered, and she stepped outside.

It was a short drive to the cemetery, then a short walk to Carl's gravesite. Cornelia ran her fingers over the name carved in the tombstone.

"I'm sorry, Carl. I love you."

Cornelia placed flowers in front of the tombstone, then she set the psalm beside the flowers.

"Thank you, Carl. For all the good times. Sixty-three years of marriage. How blessed we were. God was faithful for all those years. Why would I doubt Him now?"

Tanya took her hand, and they stood in silence, enjoying the moment.

As they walked slowly back to the car a gentle breeze began to blow.

Back in her room Cornelia turned on the computer. Gone were the feelings of anger and bitterness. She wrote:

> Little Bunny lived all alone in a cave in the
> woods. One day Little Bunny decided to see the
> world. As she stepped from the darkness into
> the brightness of the green forest, she began
> to walk and became a red fox. Her fox legs
> began to run, and the strides became great
> leaps. As she took a soaring leap, she became
> a deer, running along the paths, gliding over
> fallen logs and branches. She jumped to clear
> a large boulder, and in midair she became an
> eagle. She soared higher and higher, becoming
> a small speck on the horizon, gliding continually

upward toward the light. The light was waiting
to welcome her.

This time Cornelia did not hit delete; she hit save.

In her younger years God was good and God was
merciful. Everything was different now, but God was still
good and God was still merciful. In fact, his goodness and
mercy would follow her *all* the days of her life. The smallness of her world was only temporary. A huge world with
God was waiting for her. And one day He would walk her
home, and when he did, Carl would be waiting.

CHAPTER

Fourteen

---

*And I shall dwell in the house
of the LORD forever*

$\mathcal{A}$LARMS WENT OFF on the monitors in ICU room four.

After six weeks of slow but sure progress, Kate McConnell was in trouble. Five minutes ago everything had been normal. Dr. Belding had made rounds, and the nurses were back at the nurses' station, chatting about their evening plans. Kate's husband and son had just left for a cup of coffee.

Two nurses rushed in and checked the readings on the machines.

"BP: sixty over forty," one said. She began pushing aside unnecessary equipment. "Call a code blue."

Dr. Belding was finishing his rounds in the ICU when he heard the call.

"What are her vital signs?" he asked as he hurried into Kate's room.

Nurses were checking the monitor connections and IVs.

"BP: sixty over twenty. Pulse: one ten. Oxygen saturation: sixty."

"Ventilator pressure?"

"Normal." The nurse's voice was laced with frustration.

"Suction the trach tube," Dr. Belding said.

The nurse was already disconnecting the tube.

"Nothing—no blood or mucus," she said as she suctioned.

The resident doctor entered.

"BP dropping—forty over zero," the second nurse yelled.

"Give her more fluids," Dr. Belding said, his voice beginning to reflect some tension. "And get some meds on board."

He signaled the resident, who immediately gave instructions to the nurses. The room was a swirl of activity.

"Is there an airway problem?" the resident asked.

"No, ventilator pressures are fine."

"Heart attack?"

"No, she's too young," Dr. Belding said. "Probably a pulmonary embolism."

"But we've been giving her heparin," the resident said.

"That's no guarantee."

"Blood pressure: zero," the nurse said.

"Start CPR," Dr. Belding said. The resident was already on the bed, leaning over Kate. "And find the family."

One nurse ran from the room back to the nurses' station. She flipped through the chart, trying to find John's cell number.

The room remained eerily quiet as the resident compressed Kate's chest and one of the nurses pumped air into her lungs with the Ambu bag. Dr. Belding watched with arms crossed and brow knitted.

The compressions and pumping continued. All the while the faces of the people in the room showed their distress at the direction things were going. They had cared for Kate McConnell for six weeks now. The little blond lady on the bed was real to them, even though she had not said a single word.

Around the room the walls were covered in scripture verses. Some printed from people's computers, some written out. Many in Kate's own handwriting.

"Don't let her go," the resident said, pleading with himself.

The nurse and resident switched positions and continued compressions.

"Keep going," the nurse said, her face red from exertion.

Time seemed to stand still as they continued their silent efforts to save the woman on the bed.

Finally Dr. Belding said, "How long have we been doing this?"

The nurse checked the clock. "Forty-five minutes."

"Has there been any response on the monitor?"

The resident said, "No. No pulse. No blood pressure. No evidence of a heartbeat at all."

"Then we need to stop. She's gone."

The small crew of nurses and doctors stood still for a moment, unable to make the shift from rescue to relief.

Kate's small body lay still on the bed. Her hands rested on the quilt that she had made years ago for Matt when he was a baby. Beside the bed were flowers, many flowers from the friends and family who loved her. And cards—cards that had been taped to the wall, waiting for Kate to wake up and see how much she was loved.

"Find the family," Dr. Belding said again, and the small

group began to pack up their equipment and disperse. All was quiet.

KATE FELT RELIEF. For so long the machine had kept air moving in and out. Now it had stopped, and a sense of release and peace flowed through her. Around her were the dear people who had cared for her body so diligently over the past six weeks. She could see the sadness in their faces. She wanted to speak to them, to thank them, to encourage them, but she became aware of light shining around her. She could see the walls of the small hospital room, but above her looked like sky, open and blue.

The light shone brighter and brighter, until the hospital room disappeared and there was only light, more beautiful than anything she had ever seen. It was so bright that she wanted to look away, but so lovely that she could not. And music flowed, soft and warm, surrounding her.

The light became brighter . . . brighter . . . brighter, and suddenly Kate McConnell saw Jesus. She gazed at his beauty, like nothing she had seen or even imagined. She felt suspended and motionless before him.

She was vaguely aware of some earthly movement behind her, and she thought briefly of the two people she loved the most in the world: Matt and John.

"Will they be all right?" she asked wordlessly.

Jesus nodded.

"I'll care for them. You can come now."

Kate reached out to Jesus, and as she exhaled her last breath on earth, she was lifted into her shepherd's embrace. Her final earthly thought was the last line of the twenty-third psalm—*I shall dwell in the house of the Lord forever.*

JOHN SAT IN THE SMALL CHAPEL feeling the closeness of God. The last six weeks had been the hardest of his life. First the accident, then the weeks in ICU, and the cards and visits and endless casseroles from friends. Most of all, it was the love of Kate's church friends that moved him. Two men from her Sunday School class had brought over a freezer and set it up in the garage. Every day dinners and food appeared in the freezer. He and Matt quickly became the microwave kings.

The stories. As they sat, often for hours in the ICU waiting room, friends would stop by and pass the time. The conversation would turn to Kate and a story of a meal delivered, prayers given. One woman who had been going through chemo told how Kate had come over to clean her bathtub. Her eyes filled with tears as she related the story. John saw a different part of Kate's life—a whole support system of genuine care and love and faith.

I want that faith, too, John prayed silently. *I want to be part of that family. I want to love like that. And I want that for Matt.*

Prayer came so easily for John now. He remembered driving to the hospital that first day, unable to form any prayer in his mind. As he sat in the quiet of the chapel, he felt a closeness to God that was new and real. He could almost feel the arms of God around him, comforting him.

He took a deep breath of release.

Then his phone began to vibrate.

———————

MATT WAS IN THE GIFT SHOP when his phone rang. His father.

"Yes," he said into the phone.

"You better come up to the room. Something's happened. The nurse just called."

"What?"

"They didn't say. Come up right away."

Matt took the stairs two at a time. He pushed open the door into ICU and saw the crash cart and the faces of the team. Dr. Belding stood outside the room, shaking his head, talking to John.

He ran the last steps to the room.

His father's strong hands grabbed his shoulders.

"She's gone, Matt. She's gone."

Matt could not move. He could not go in the room. The world had just shifted and would never be the same.

"No."

His father's arms wrapped around him and held him tight.

Father and son stood in the embrace, leaning on a strength outside of themselves.

———————

FOR KATE, time was gone. Space was gone. Jesus was everything.

She gazed down at the world. The picture looked so

much bigger than she had imagined. As she stood beside Jesus with his view of the world, she could see so much.

A young man stood beside a girl who was wearing a red beret. It was Chris from the dry cleaner's! He and the girl were singing songs of praise in a worship service not too far from where Kate lived. The smiles on their faces spoke of an abundant life with God. On the girl's finger was an engagement ring.

Kate smiled with joy at the transformation she saw in the young man.

She turned to another scene.

A soldier was resting on his crutches, knocking at the front door of a ranch house in North Carolina. The door opened, and an older couple spoke to the man, then embraced him. The spirit of comfort and peace hovered around the three, and tears flowed freely as the soldier shared with them stories of their son, Tater, and his testimony of faith.

Next, Kate saw a young girl in Turkey, running to pick up the mail. The girl's face reflected the freedom and excitement of knowing the true God for the first time. She ripped open her package and pulled out a book. Immediately she opened it and read, in her own language, the title: *The Holy Bible*. She quickly turned to Psalm 23 and read verse two. *He leads me beside still waters.* Her eyes filled with tears of joy, and she hugged the Bible to her chest.

A Frenchman appeared. He was standing in an art gallery in England, staring at a painting titled *The Good Shepherd*. The man's face reflected peace and joy as he pointed to the gate and the sheep and enthusiastically discussed the painting with his friend. They laughed and talked of all kinds of restoration.

Kate saw the hills and dales of Ireland—an idyllic setting with miles and miles of pastureland filled with sheep. A young redheaded man in the field leaned down to kiss the small baby in the sling wrapped around his chest. The man tenderly led the sheep down the path to home, all the while holding tight to the baby.

Jesus turned to Kate. "Do you understand?"

Kate looked at him, unsure.

"The twenty-third psalm. You sent it out," He said. "So is my word that goes out from my mouth: It will not return to me empty, but will accomplish what I desire and achieve the purpose for which I sent it."

Kate marveled at all the people, living in the power of Psalm 23. They flashed before her in scene after scene, and she knew it was a result of the copy of the psalm that she had so carefully written and prayed over.

"Your word," she said. "It was all about your word."

"There's more," Jesus said.

A small urban church appeared. A minister was preaching about walking through valleys. He spoke with authority and conviction, as if he himself had been through a valley. His wife looked on, as did a full house of the poor and needy who were thankful to have him.

In the next scene a young woman with many tattoos sat in the front row of a church. She sang with the congregation, her arms lifted heavenward. Her face was set with confidence as she sang. The music ended, and the girl stepped forward. She gave her testimony with power and courage. Other young women listened eagerly to her words, needing her hope.

Kate's heart was full to a point she had never experienced on earth. She praised Jesus over and over as the scenes continued.

A scene of Africa unfolded, a young woman running down the red dirt road as a huge orange sun rose over the plains. She ran fearlessly and confidently. Young girls ran beside her, trying to keep up. As she ran on, they stopped and spoke to one another. "We can be like Kioni one day. God takes care of her. He can take care of us, too."

Then Kate saw a large Italian family gathered around a long wooden table. The older gentleman sitting at the head of the table was holding the hands of his wife on one side and his brother on the other. "And we thank you for once again watching out for the Liberatores," he said, and he squeezed the hand of his brother.

A young Chinese student entered the doors of a church in Los Angeles for the first time. Several other Chinese students moved forward to greet her. In her own language they began to tell her about the God who anoints and protects.

In a small restaurant in New York City a businessman sat with his daughter, talking about all the blessings in their lives. The man was laughing as he told the story of his cross-country flight with a woman named Judy, who had opened his eyes to what makes a person's cup overflow. His cell phone rang. Without looking at the phone he hit the silence button and shoved it in his pocket. He and his daughter left the restaurant arm in arm.

Finally, a white-haired woman sitting at her computer was printing out a finished document. Suddenly she stopped and grabbed her chest. The woman's eyes grew large with amazement, and Kate knew exactly what she was seeing.

"Walk me home now, Jesus," the woman said. Then her eyes closed. A moment later the woman, glowing and radiant, moved past Kate. "Carl," she said moving toward a man who was also glowing. Their joy was supernatural. Kate knew that feeling.

"So many," Kate said. "So many."

As she watched, the view expanded. There were thousands of cards, her copies of scriptures, all over the city, all over the country, all over the world.

"I never knew," she said in amazement. "I never dreamed."

"There's one more," Jesus said.

"One more?" Kate asked. It was already so much more than she had imagined.

Jesus pointed, and Kate turned to see her own son, Matt.

A BREEZE RUFFLED MATT'S HAIR as he stood beside his mother's grave. His father's hand rested on his shoulder. Matt was wearing his navy peacoat, and his face was streaked with tears. Dry leaves blew by, and the air was warm for December.

Matt knelt and touched the flowers in front of the stone.

"I'm sorry, Mom," he said. "I'm sorry, God. Give me one more chance."

He wondered if God could hear him. He hadn't cared about God in so long. He used to be indifferent, then so angry. Now he was just sorry. If only he could talk to his mother one more time.

"Just one more chance," he repeated, looking up at the dark clouds above.

He thought of his mother and all that she had wanted for him. If only he had another chance to tell her, yes—to tell God yes.

Matt was staring at his mother's name, so neatly etched on the headstone, when the wind began to swirl. Some leaves blew by, and out of the corner of his eye, Matt saw a flash of white. It was a piece of paper, tumbling across the graveyard toward him. He paused, mesmerized by the moving paper—the gentle way it curled and rolled and took on a life of its own. Then the paper whirled up and caught on the edge of the roughly hewn headstone of his mother's grave.

Matt stared at the paper. He couldn't explain why, but he knew it was for him. With calm anticipation, he reached out and took the paper. It was worn and crumpled and badly stained with what looked like blood and oil and water—maybe even grass or coffee. When he flipped the paper over, he could barely breathe. Written neatly across the top, in his mother's handwriting, were the words *The Shepherd's Song, Psalm 23.*

How could it be? Where had it come from? Matt looked around in amazement. He saw no one. He lifted his eyes up to the sun emerging from the clouds and let the rays warm his face. Peace washed over him.

"Dad," he called. "Dad, look."

John knelt beside Matt, and together they looked at the paper.

Matt began to read, pausing with each line.

The LORD is my shepherd;
I shall not want.
He makes me lie down in green pastures.
He leads me beside still waters.
He restores my soul.
He leads me in paths of righteousness
    for his name's sake.
Even though I walk through the valley of the shadow
    of death,
I will fear no evil,
for you are with me;
your rod and staff, they comfort me.
You prepare a table before me in the presence of my
    enemies;
you anoint my head with oil;
    my cup overflows.
Surely goodness and mercy shall follow me
    all the days of my life.

He stopped. He could not read the last line. He was overwhelmed. His mother was with Jesus "in the house of the Lord." He remembered her peace and the strength of her faith.

"Yes, Jesus," he said. "I want you to be my shepherd."

It was as if the clock had turned back to that moment six weeks ago when he had first pulled the psalm from the pocket of his coat.

"Thank you, Mom," he said to the grave. "The Lord *is* my shepherd."

He looked again at the paper. The psalm was different from the last time he'd read it. Yet it wasn't. They were the same words as before, only now *he* was different. The arrogance was gone—his anger and sadness had evaporated. He was hearing with new ears.

He looked up and said, "Mom, this is what you wanted me to know all along—the Lord is my shepherd." And he knew it was true.

HIGH ABOVE, Kate finished the last line of the psalm for him, "'And I shall dwell in the house of the Lord forever.'"

Her joy was complete. Her work on earth, done.

"Well done, good and faithful servant," Jesus said.

Kate remembered praying, "Let my life count," and she knew her prayer had been answered.

She turned from the earthly scenes and took the hand of Jesus, ready to dwell in the house of the Lord forever.

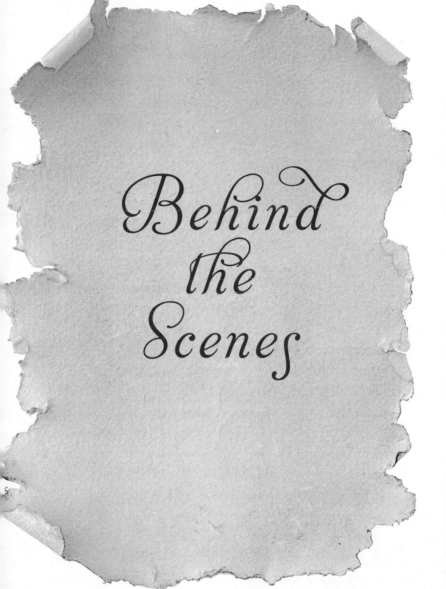

Behind
the
Scenes

The Shepherd's Song began in a small coffee shop in Madison, Georgia, when we met and prayed for God to reveal our next writing project.

We had been meeting at Perk Avenue, a coffee shop halfway between our homes, one day a week for more than a year and had made the decision to use our years of writing skills and publishing experience for God.

The idea for *The Shepherd's Song* was different from what we had done before. Betsy had read Psalm 23 that morning and was drawn to the thought of how that scripture could change lives. We discussed the challenge of writing this book for adults, since our previous experiences had been in children's books and it wasn't something we knew how to do. We knew we would have to rely on God, which seemed perfect in light of the whole premise of Psalm 23.

The writing process turned out to be quite different from what we were used to. In previous books we had worked on separate chapters, compiling the book at the end. This time we gave each other access to our writing and worked together in a true collaboration. In the story of François, Laurie used her research skills to write the details about the work of an art restorer in Paris. Betsy, drawing on her counseling experience, layered in the story of François's wife and his grief over her death. Together we edited and refined, and the layering and surrender went on throughout the process. By the end, we could no longer even distinguish our individual voices.

We discovered early on that we had to have spiritual agreement to have unity on the page. In collaboration there will be differences of opinion, which are good and bring growth and depth to the work. It is in the resolution of the disagreements that our faith is exercised. Staying in harmony with God kept us in harmony with each other. As we constantly tried to align our work with God's will, we aligned ourselves with each other, and the story gradually became more than it would have been otherwise, something truly special.

Acknowledgments

WHEN YOU BEGIN a new direction, especially with the intent of pointing people in the direction of God, you need divine help. First and foremost we give thanks to God for guiding and inspiring us with every aspect of this book. He lifted us in times of doubt, gave us confidence in times of insecurity, and put up with us in times of rebellion. Praise to Him.

We are fortunate to have husbands who have supported and loved us for more than thirty-five years each. Thank you, Bill and Michael. Thank you also to our parents, Ed and Betsy Byars, who have cheered us on in every endeavor.

We prayed for a team for this book, and God graciously provided just the right people.

First, our agent, Greg Johnson, who at a luncheon for hundreds chose an empty seat beside us. His confidence, encouragement, and experience as a literary agent were an important part of this book.

From her very first email we liked our editor, Jessica Wong. She is a wonderful combination of encouragement, insight, and guidance. Thank you, Jessica, and all the talented people at Howard Books.

Accuracy was of utmost importance to us when writing about other cultures. We are grateful to those who added their own expertise to the details: Dr. Michael Hawkins, Debbie Hawkins, Jeremy Rueggeberg, Tony DiRenzo, Anthony Giardino, June Murakaru, and Toufic Azar.

Finally, the team would not be complete without the hundreds of friends, family members, and colleagues who have been part of our prayer team. Your prayers and support have made this possible.

Thank you all.

About the Authors

BETSY DUFFEY AND LAURIE MYERS were born into a writing family. Their father wrote engineering textbooks and magazine articles; their mother, Betsy Byars, was a distinguished children's author and the winner of numerous book awards, including a National Book Award, a Newbery, an Edgar, and many others.

They grew up in Morgantown, West Virginia, and after careers in medical fields they both began writing. For over twenty years they published more than thirty-five children's novels with a variety of companies, both individually and together.

Their first collaborative efforts were with their mother. When their mother retired, Laurie and Betsy formed The Writing Sisters to express their faith in their writing and more directly use their talents for the glory of God. Their desire is for their fiction to show the power of God working in the world through scripture.

A Howard Reading Group Guide

The
Shepherd's
Song

Betsy Duffey and Laurie Myers

Introduction

The Shepherd's Song tells the story of Kate McConnell and her unparalleled faith in God's master plan. The day before suffering a terrible car accident, Kate copies, by hand, Psalm 23 for her wayward son, Matt. This little piece of paper makes its way around the world, touching the lives of twelve distinct individuals, all in need of God's powerful words. In the end, the psalm makes its way back into Matt's hands, bringing the story full circle and fulfilling Kate's mission to spread God's love.

Questions for Discussion

1. The story of *The Shepherd's Song* begins with Psalm 23 on page xi. Reread the psalm aloud to your group. How does the psalm act as a framework for the novel? What is Kate's relationship to the psalm? What is yours? If you could summarize Psalm 23's message in just one sentence, what would it be?

2. "She felt the ambulance sway, then the jolt of a sharp turn. 'Help.' Kate gasped again as pain stabbed through her side. 'Stay with me.' A wave of dizziness.

Then nothing" (5–6). Return to this opening scene in the ambulance. What first impression does Kate make on you? How would you characterize her?

3. When John McConnell learns of his wife's accident, his reaction is one of determination: "There will be a way to fix this. There is always a way to fix things" (13). Do you agree with John's statement? Discuss the ways in which what he says is true and the ways in which he is wrong.

4. Discuss how second chances are a theme for the novel. Who gets a second chance in *The Shepherd's Song*? Who doesn't?

5. On page 20 Kate's last thought is revealed: *Please, let my life count.* What do you think Kate meant by saying this? In your opinion, is her last wish realized?

6. How would you describe John and Matt McConnell? How would their lives be different without Kate? Use one word to describe the impact Kate had on her husband and son.

7. "There was something almost irresistible about nice clothes. It was like he could become someone else, someone worthy" (25). In what ways does borrowing Matt McConnell's peacoat change Chris's life?

8. On page 71, François wonders aloud to himself, "But how in the world do you restore a soul?" Answer François's question, using examples of times in your life when you felt your soul needed restoring.

9. The sight of his newborn son turns Patrick's life around. Revisit the scene of Patrick's homecoming on page 87–88, taking note of the many ways in which Patrick realizes God's love all around him. Why do you think children so often bring about such realizations in life? Has this happened to you?

10. Why do you think Marra chooses to tell her life story through tattoos? If you were to summarize your life in an image, what would it be and why?

11. To which story did you most relate? Which story touched you the most? Why?

12. Discuss the ending chapter of *The Shepherd's Song*. On what note does the story that began this book, end? What are the most poignant lessons you take away from the book?

Additional Activities: Ways of Enhancing Your Book Club

1. On page 168, Judy describes her Thanksgiving traditions to Roland, making his mouth water in the process. Host a faux Thanksgiving dinner with your book club. Have each member bring a dish that is important to his or her Thanksgiving tradition. Over dinner, have each member share a personal recipe and why that particular dish is so important to him or her. Take a moment to thank God for the many ways in

which your own cup runs over, and after, discuss with your book club Roland's encounter with Judy. Has there ever been a "Judy" in your life?

2. Cornelia's short story about Little Bunny gives a lot of insight into her own life and character. Reread Cornelia's short story on pages 188–189. Then have each member write his or her own "Little Bunny story," using Cornelia's as a model. Share the stories out loud with the group; explain how your story reflects some aspect of your life.

3. Continue in the vein of *The Shepherd's Song* by reading either Andy Andrews's *The Butterfly Effect* or his *The Traveler's Gift*. What common theme can be found in the two novels you've read? How does each touch on the notion of faith changing the world?

Author Q&A with Betsy Duffey and Laurie Myers

1. *The two of you are seasoned children's book authors, but this novel marks your debut into the world of adult fiction. What are the differences between writing for children and writing for adults? Is one more challenging than the other?*

   BETSY: There are more similarities than differences. Everyone likes a good story, and although the themes may be more advanced for adults, the basics are the same—tell a good story and tell it simply.

   LAURIE: Our years of writing for children helped us

to hone our skills. Children are a discerning audience, and they detect any trace of the artificial. To keep a child turning pages requires an economy of words and a constant reward of action as the story moves forward. These are things that adults like, too.

2. *What is it like to co-author a book? You touch on this question briefly on page 206, but it would be wonderful to hear more about the writing process and how the work is divided between the two of you.*

BETSY: We use a common document online that we can both access, so either of us can make changes at anytime. We've found this to be much more convenient than sending attachments back and forth by email and ending up with multiple copies of the manuscript.

LAURIE: Usually one of us will start a story; the other will then jump in and add some backstory, or another character, or a plot twist. It's fun to go into the document and read what's new.

This method also requires trust. Twenty years of publishing experience has helped. We both have worked with a variety of editors, so we've learned how to let go of passages and ideas.

BETSY: The interaction makes it fun. This is how it goes:

The phone rings.

"Hey."

"I have some bad news."

"What?"

"I just killed Cornelia."

"No! You can't kill Cornelia."

"Sorry, it just happened."

LAURIE: Or sometimes . . .

"Hey."

"Hey, guess what? Chris is engaged!"

"What?! Our Chris? To the girl in the red beret?"

"Oh, I'm so happy for him."

3. *You write that as sisters you meet often to pray about your next book project. Briefly describe the power of prayer in your lives and how prayer and faith are tied into your careers as writers.*

LAURIE: Prayer makes collaboration possible . . . especially as sisters. We are both different people with different personalities, but we have the same God. As we both surrender our work to God, we come into alignment with each other.

BETSY: We discovered early in our attempts to write together that when we prayed, we could remove our egos from the writing and allow God to work through us together.

4. *On page 179 the character Cornelia writes that "writer's block was simply fear." Do you two agree?*

BETSY: You caught us being ourselves! Cornelia was a fun character because we could tap into our own fears and insecurities as writers.

LAURIE: Most writers struggle with fear—fear of failure, rejection, exposure, even fear of success. Writing authentically requires courage. You have to be willing to be vulnerable and open yourself up to the possibilities of rejection. Cornelia was also fun, because we were able to show her conquer her fear—a hope we have for us all!

5. *What would you name as the major theme(s) of this novel? Is there a lesson you hope readers will take away from this story?*

LAURIE: There are so many powerful themes that flow from the twenty-third Psalm. God's deep love and care for us and His protection and blessing. The idea of second chances permeates the book. God is constantly seeking us and restoring us.

BETSY: As we read scripture we are continually called into second chances, to start over again like Roland, to heal like François, to restore relationships like Patrick, to begin to know God like Matt. No matter what has happened in our lives or what we have done, God is always ready to welcome us back into the fold.

6. The Shepherd's Song *is about so many different people in so many different situations. Does the format of this story represent our shared story as human beings living together on the same planet?*

BETSY: Although Zoey was Chinese, there are students all over the world who leave their homes to go to other countries for educational experiences; and although François was French, men and women everywhere lose spouses to cancer. And across the world women are in abusive situations, people lose jobs, deal with loss, estranged relationships, discouragement.

LAURIE: The issues in *The Shepherd's Song* are universal issues, and the beauty of the Bible is that it crosses cultures to heal and give hope in all life situations.

7. *Were any of the characters based on people you have known? On historical figures? On yourself?*

BETSY: Characters are multilayered, and the different layers come from different places. Physical traits can come from someone we know or a stranger we spot on the street. Personality traits can also come from people we know or someone we read about in the paper.

LAURIE: Sometimes characters just come straight out of our heads, with no connection to anyone.

BETSY: The feelings of the characters come from our own experiences. Grief, pain, love, shame, and fear all are in some way and at different levels common experiences for everyone.

LAURIE: During the writing of a story characters evolve, and quickly they become real people to us.

8. *What was it like writing about characters from so many different cultural backgrounds? How do you go about doing this authentically?*

LAURIE: More than writing about cultures, we were writing about people. A Kenyan runner running across the plains of Africa. An olive grower looking out over the Bay of Naples. A wounded soldier in a hospital in Iraq. These were all people, people in different settings. Reflecting the culture authentically was important to us.

BETSY: There is so much diversity within our own

communities that we found we had, right around us, many resources to draw from. Each story that reflected a different culture was read and critiqued by a person of that culture.

9. *Why Psalm 23? What special place does this particular psalm hold in your hearts? What important message do you each find in this psalm?*

BETSY: We both remember this psalm from childhood, in the King James version. Although we used a more modern translation in *The Shepherd's Song*, the old words still resonated with us. In our minds He still leadeth and restoreth us!

LAURIE: Psalm 23 is the most well-known scripture passage in the Bible. The challenge for us was to look at these familiar words in fresh ways and imagine how God could work in a person's life through each phrase.

BETSY: As we studied the psalm and meditated on the truth behind the words we developed a different understanding. Psalm 23 is such a beautiful picture of shepherd's role and therefore God's role in our lives.

LAURIE: From the opening line "The Lord is my shepherd," where God is confirmed as completely in control; and throughout each line where he is looking out for our well-being and loving us sacrificially; to the final line with a remarkable promise of dwelling with Him forever.

10. *What's next for the two of you as writers?*

LAURIE: When we showed up at the coffee shop two years ago and prayed "Here I am," we began a journey that took us into writing *The Shepherd's Song*. We love the idea that through fiction you can show how holy words can heal and give hope and change lives.

BETSY: As long as God continues to give us ideas, we will continue to write.